God for... her, to shed his own grief and distract her from hers.

With his conscience shouting that it was wrong, that it would be unforgivable to take advantage, he drowned out his body's protests.

But before he could step back, she arched her neck to look up into his eyes and ran her fingers along the light stubble on his jaw. "Jake," she whispered.

His name was all it took for him to dip his mouth to hers, to taste the lips he'd dreamed of night after lonely night. And in that instant he felt whole again, an unscarred young man with the world and all its possibilities laid out before him like a feast.

Dear Reader,

Is there any instinct more powerful than a mother's drive to keep her children safe, or a man's need to protect his family—even if it's only the family of his heart?

As a mother, I am all too able to imagine myself going to extremes, just as single mom Liane Mason is forced to do when her children and her aging father go missing in the Yosemite-area wilderness one stormy summer night. And as the wife of a firefighter, I'm all too well acquainted with the dangers lightning can touch off under those conditions.

Still emotionally fragile from the violent abuse that drove her back to her hometown, Liane has forgotten how to trust anyone. It's a lucky thing for her that former hotshot firefighter Jake Whittaker, her first love, who's never been able to forget her, isn't the type to take no for an answer.

I hope you'll enjoy this dangerous journey into the California backcountry with a courageous woman and a hero I couldn't help but fall in love with. Thanks to my editors and everyone at Harlequin Books for helping me bring this story to life!

Happy reading,

Colleen Thompson

COLLEEN THOMPSON

Passion to Protect

HARLEQUIN®
entertain, enrich, inspire™

ISBN-13: 978-0-373-27799-5

PASSION TO PROTECT

Books by Rachel Lee

Harlequin Romantic Suspense

Passion to Protect #1729

Silhouette Romantic Suspense

Deadlier Than the Male #1631
  "Lethal Lessons"

Harlequin Intrigue

Capturing the Commando #1286
Phantom of the French Quarter #1302
Relentless Protector #1376

COLLEEN THOMPSON

After beginning her career writing historical romance novels, in 2004 Colleen Thompson turned to writing the contemporary romantic suspense she loves. Since then, her work has been honored with a Texas Gold Award, along with nominations for a RITA® Award, a Daphne du Maurier Award and multiple reviewers' choice honors. She has also received starred reviews from *RT Book Reviews* and *Publishers Weekly.* A former teacher living with her family in the Houston area, Colleen has a passion for reading, hiking and dog rescue. Visit her online at www.colleen-thompson.com.

To all those who risk their hearts—and sometimes their lives—to protect the powerless.

Prologue

If politics made strange bedfellows, prison breaks made far worse ones. But Mac McCleary, who hadn't gone by his given name in decades, had seen no other way out than to promise each participant a cut.

That promise, he feared, was about to cost him his life.

Outside the hollow shell of one of several dilapidated cabins, all three of his coconspirators glared at him: the Mexican called Goose, who had been the one with the connections inside; the cadaverous, balding AK, who provided both the brains and plans; and most frightening of all, Smash, who had offered the muscle and the intimidation factor, not to mention a pair of skanks on the outside with an almost religious need to prove themselves to the convicted murderer.

As a dry wind rattled its way through the parched pine boughs overhead, Mac reminded himself that *he* had been the linchpin, the only man with both the story and the discipline to weave four antisocial convicts into one cohesive unit. A unit he had lost control of the moment he discovered that the lure he had dangled was gone.

"It was all bull, wasn't it?" demanded Smash, the skinheaded mountain of a man he'd been initially horrified to have as a cell mate. The fury smoldering in his tiny, dark eyes promised the explosion Mac had spent the past few years avoiding. "The whole freakin' fairy tale was nothin' but a scam, first to keep me off your ass and then to bust you out. While you planned all along to ditch us first chance you got."

"I swear," Mac told them, looking from one man to the next, "that was never the idea."

Ignoring his denial, the nearly mute AK glared, while Goose looked up coolly from where he'd been paring his nails with a fifteen-inch hunting knife, part of the haul from the sporting goods store they'd hit on their first night out before heading for the California state line. "That's where you're wrong, *Gringo*. Only one who's gettin' ditched is you. Except we might be leaving you in a hell of a lot more pieces than you figured."

Sweat dampening his stolen clothing, Mac raised his palms. "Wait a minute, guys. It's gotta be the old man. Looks to me like he's fixed up the old bunkhouse. Who's to say he hasn't been digging around under those rotten floors in the other cabins?"

"But you told us the money's never been found," Smash said. "You said you hid it so well, there's no way it never would be."

"It's never been *reported* found," Mac amended, "but why would the old man report it if he could take it for himself? Bastard never did like me."

Mac turned to glare at the big, two-story log lodge—referred to as the homestead, since it had been in his ex-wife's family for generations. In far better shape than the outbuildings, the Yosemite-area landmark stood proudly as a refuge for the ex-wife who'd never understood that everything he'd done, he'd done for his family. Instead she had betrayed him, walking into open court and saying all those things about him, things that had been used to put him in a cage, where he'd been forced to scramble for survival among lowlife rats.

"He decide he hated your ass before or after you shot his little girl?" The hairless mountain—whose own mama had been beaten to death by her boyfriend—had never made any secret of his contempt for Mac's crime, but this time, as the huge man scowled down, violence gathered like a storm behind his coal-black eyes.

Mac fought the temptation to take a step backward. If he turned to run, they would be on him in a second, and his gut contracted as he imagined the things they would likely to do to him before he died. "I'll find it, I swear to you. He must've moved it, that's all, and you mark my words, it'll be around here somewhere. Whenever I tried talking to him about investing in securities, that old gasbag was always saying how the Mason Ranch and Homestead were all the security he needed."

AK, who had injured his leg in the escape, limped closer and finally spoke up, menace freezing his words solid. "So let's go have a talk with him, then, shall we?"

They had already knocked at the door and looked around enough to know the lodge was empty, and Mac didn't find him in the stable, either. Panic thumping in his chest, he almost forgot to check out the dry-erase board, the one where the sanctimonious old John Wayne wannabe had written out a message to any potential customers who stopped by:

Howdy, partners!

On an overnight trip to Elk Creek Canyon with the grandkids.

Expected return: Friday at 4:00 p.m.

To schedule *your* Equine Adventure, call 1-559-555-6840!

Deke

Smash cursed, "Hell, man. I don't wanta cool my heels around here waiting for him. You said yourself, once the Nevada cops catch up with the girls and figure out we're not the ones runnin' up those charges or usin' that old geezer's cell phone, this'll be the first place they come looking."

As a plan came to him, Mac felt a slow smile pulling back his lips. "No need to wait the old man out. I've suffered through my share of camping trips with him and my ex, and I remember the way to Elk Creek Canyon just fine."

"Back in all them woods? That what you talkin', *padre?*" Looking past the horses in the corral, Goose sounded dubious—or nervous—and the injured AK crossed his arms, looking even more miserable.

"Aw, come on, boys," Mac said, eager to be the man in charge again and knowing only one sure way to do it. On his terms, on his turf. "How 'bout the four of us go on a little equine adventure of our own?"

Chapter 1

The dark silhouettes of pine trees swirled around Liane Mason, the evening sky behind them as red as fresh-spilled blood. Behind the wheel of her parked Jeep, she was shaking so hard she barely managed to slip her phone back inside her purse.

Closing her eyes, she gulped down several deep breaths, allowing the crisp mountain air to remind her that there were a hundred different reasons, benign reasons, why her father might not be answering either his cell phone or the radio, and just as many why the kids weren't, either.

More than likely eight-year-old Cody and his six-year-old sister Kenzie were outside, helping their grandfather put away the tack and camping supplies they had taken on their first overnight horseback excursion. His business might be a far cry from the carefully manicured and wildly successful Wolf River Lodge and Spa, where she spent her days managing the needs of wealthy and sometimes-famous clients, but Deke Mason had been known for decades for the personalized guided trail rides he'd offered generations of tourists of all stripes. Though his business had fallen off in recent years, he had safely and successfully taken thousands in and out of Elk Creek Canyon. Well trained in first aid, he was carrying the kit that contained Kenzie's medication—and Liane trusted him to deal with anything that came up.

So there was absolutely no reason to believe that he'd had any trouble this time. No logical reason to allow her smoldering panic to ignite. But that line of thought didn't ease her worry for a moment, regardless of anything her post-traumatic-stress counselor had told her.

You could always call Jake Whittaker, have him go outside and check. But the thought of asking a favor of her dad's new tenant, who had taken up residence in the rebuilt bunkhouse about six months before his accident last summer, stopped her. Though she knew Jake would insist on going out to check, she hated to think of him walking the uneven ground, maybe missing his footing in the deep drifts of rust-colored pine needles, thicker than ever thanks to what had been the driest summer in a decade.

She shook her head, realizing she was lying to herself. Prosthetic leg or not, Jake was getting around fine these days, just over a year after the accident and amputation. More than fine, considering the glimpses she'd caught of him toweling sweat from his body after a run—a body even more buff and masculine than when the two of them had dated back in high school.

Awkward as it had been facing the boy she'd left behind—facing the whole town of Mill Falls—since her return last fall, the truth was that she had no intention of admitting exactly how close to melting down she was right now. Now that she'd finished her busy shift, she could be home in twenty minutes, anyway.

She visualized herself arriving at the big, comfortable log homestead and hugging her kids close. As they excitedly chattered about the trip they had been begging her to let them take all summer, her dad would grin and tell her how proud his family made him. And his eyes would meet hers in silent acknowledgment that he was proudest of all that she had made it through the night alone....

Or as alone as a woman *could* be, with her father's seventy-pound shepherd mix hogging most of the bed. But since Misty could be trusted to keep a secret, Liane wouldn't mention the sleepless hours she'd spent stroking the shaggy, blue-gray head and praying for the night to pass more quickly.

As she drove along the tree-lined highway that skirted Bear Mountain, she told herself she would catch up on her sleep tonight. Safe at home, they all would, nestled in their beds.

Focusing on that image, she relaxed her death grip on the wheel and consciously deepened her breathing. It was enough to get her through the drive home.

And enough to distract her from the teasing flicker of the gathering darkness illuminated by summer lightning in her rearview.

The night cried out for flame. As Jake Whittaker stood on the porch of his mountain valley cabin, he heard it in the hiss of hot wind through the drought-scorched treetops, the creak of trunks so parched and resinous that the slightest spark would send them up, and the restless nickers of the horses that milled about his friend and landlord Deke's corral a short distance downhill.

But most of all he felt it in the phantom ache in the lower

left leg he'd lost: the warning that a storm was brewing. A
dry electrical storm that would light up the backcountry
near Yosemite in time to choke the dawn with thick smoke.

Last year's accident, the result of a tree whose fall had
knocked Jake out of his fire boots as he'd been racing to
the aid of his trapped men, had nearly killed him, but there
was nothing wrong with his instincts, which had his blood
quickening and his pulse thrumming with the first flicker
of heat lightning along the ridge to the west. Though he
now spent the better part of most of his days at a computer
translating scientific articles and tech support documents
into the Russian he'd learned at his grandmother's knee, it
was still everything he could do not to jump into his truck
and join the crew of hotshot firefighters he had once led—
firefighters, he reluctantly admitted, whose effectiveness
and safety would be jeopardized if he were selfish and
foolhardy enough to try.

For now, at least, he told himself. But maybe by next
summer's fire season, if he worked hard enough to convince the district supervisors…

Another flicker pulsed behind Bear Mountain, and
thunder rumbled a dark warning. From the corral, he heard
a terrified equine squeal, followed by deep barking and a
frantic female cry.

"Copper, stand still! Please!"

Jake reached inside the front door for a flashlight and
was on the move an instant later, driven by the desperation in Liane Mason's voice. Something had to be wrong
for the woman he'd once known so well to be out messing
with the horses after dark. He hadn't been raised around
the animals as Liane had, but even he knew that both the
weather and the panic in her voice would do nothing but
upset them. What could have happened to make the Ice
Princess forget that?

As he threaded his way through the trees, Jake's prosthesis caught a branch buried in leaf litter. Cursing the hurry that had made him lose his focus on his footing, he recovered from his stumble, then gritted his teeth and hurried toward the security light just outside the stable.

Beneath it, he spotted the woman it still hurt to look at, even a dozen years after she had dashed his naive schoolboy fantasies and kicked him to the curb. As slender and agile as she'd been at eighteen, she was struggling to saddle a horse, her long brown braid whipping along the back of the chambray shirt she wore hanging over her jeans. As the dog paced nervously, the muscular bay danced sideways, tossing his head to throw his weight against the lead rope that bound him to the hitching post. Even from this distance, Jake could make out the whites of the horse's rolling eyes.

"Put that saddle down and back off." Though it wasn't his place, he made it an order, too concerned for her safety to do any less. "He's about to break loose, and you're going to end up hurt."

Liane whirled toward him, her face milk-pale and her beautiful blue eyes huge with terror. "I have to," she said, all traces of her usual coolness toward him absent. "I have to go and find them."

"Find who, Liane?" he asked, but already he was putting the pieces together. How Cody, the outgoing and talkative second grader, had been jabbering nonstop for the past week about the planned adventure to anyone who would listen, including the tenant his mother so consistently avoided. How her father had taken her kids out on two of the gentler horses for a camping trip yesterday. How Deke's favorite mount, a huge black mule named Waco, remained as absent from the corral as the children's horses.

"Did your dad radio you?" Jake asked, knowing that

cell phone coverage didn't extend into Elk Creek Canyon. "Has there been an accident?"

Liane shook her head. "I haven't been able to raise him since this morning. He did have some issues with his satellite radio a few weeks back, but something has to be wrong. He knew how nervous I was about this trip, how I wasn't sure the kids were ready for—" A shaft of lightning interrupted, stabbing the darkness behind the mountain's granite dome. Moments later thunder reverberated through the valley, more ominous than ever.

The noise was the last straw for the bay, who squealed and launched himself backward, snapping not the lead rope but one of the bands of his own halter. As the horse wheeled around to join the herd in the corral, Liane leaped backward, holding the saddle before her like a shield.

"Help me catch another one," she demanded. "I have to find my family. Dry as it's been, there'll be fires, maybe even worse than last year's."

He nodded grimly, trying not to remember the blaze whose uncharacteristic behavior had engulfed thousands of acres, fifteen homes and the lives of three Wolf River Hotshots—three good men, family men—he'd ordered into what should have been a safe location. They were gone, but the flashbacks were always waiting, resurfacing to accuse him every time he closed his eyes.

"Let's not get ahead of ourselves. Have you called the sheriff's office yet? Or how 'bout search and rescue?" he asked.

But he was talking to her back, because she had already turned to grab a rope and a bucket of oats to sweeten the deal.

"I just got off the phone with them." With Misty sticking close by her side, Liane jogged toward the dozen or so horses trotting a nervous circle around the corral's outer edge. Their varied hides, brown and black and white and golden, streamed past the security light in a dust-choked, multicolored river. "They're refusing to send anyone 'til first light. By that time, anything could happen. Anything might have already."

He shook his head. "Elk Creek Canyon's a treacherous ride at the best of times, and you think you're going to do it on a panicked horse at this hour? You can't go out there tonight, or at least you can't go alone."

"I don't recall asking your opinion." She turned abruptly, her gaze snapping to meet his. Her stunning blue eyes went ice-cold, the way they always did around him, regardless of his every attempt to act as if he'd forgotten all about their history, as if the memory of how it ended hadn't been eating away at him since the day he'd learned that she was coming back…the day he'd first begun to realize that he'd never completely gotten past her—or his foolish orphan's dream of someday, finally, creating a family of his own.

"Listen, Liane. I get that I'm not your favorite person."

Though Deke had made it clear the subject was off-limits, Jake had heard the rumors that the life Liane had chosen hadn't gone the way she'd planned, that the man she'd married had abused her. Still, that was no reason for her to treat his every word and gesture like poison. Or to confuse him further by leaving foil-wrapped home-baked treats on his cabin porch and then slinking away before he had the chance to thank her. "Put the past aside for a minute and listen to me on this, or you're going to end up injured. And what good would that do your family?"

She stilled, her stare heating in an instant. "The past? This isn't about you, Jake. It's about my family. I'm not leaving them out there, especially on a night like this one. I can't."

He nodded, understanding her worry. He knew Deke as well as he knew anyone, had looked up to Liane's father from the first time the older man had promised to kick his backside over the nearest mountaintop if he did anything to hurt his girl. But Jake had never known him to be so long out of contact or this overdue returning from a trip.

"Then let me come with you," he offered. "It'll be a whole lot safer. I know the area well enough, and I'm used to navigating these woods night and day. I could help you pick up the trail."

A lariat looped above her head before she launched it in a smooth arc. Instead of roping the still-spooked Copper, she pulled a solidly built pinto from the herd—a herd he thought looked smaller than it should have.

Had Deke taken extra mounts for pack animals? He tried to remember how many horses he'd seen in the corral this morning on his way out for a follow-up visit with his orthopedic surgeon.

Liane held the bucket for the brown-and-white mare and led her toward the post, distracting him by saying, "But you can't possibly, with your leg—"

"The hell I can't," he ground out through clenched teeth. Before his accident he'd been in peak form, and ever since, he'd worked out daily, never allowing himself to give way to self-pity for a moment. He might have lost the career that had defined him, but three other deserving men, family men, had lost their lives last summer. "It doesn't take two legs to ride a damned horse."

Abruptly stopping in her tracks, she turned to look at him, her eyes gleaming. "I'm sorry, Jake. I know how rude that must've sounded, and I really do appreciate your offer. But we're talking about my kids and my father, and I've already wasted so much time with people on the phone.

Besides, I've been wandering these canyons since I was a kid. I can find my way blindfolded."

"You say that now, but I can tell you, no matter how well you think you know the territory, the darkness is disorienting. So saddle up a mount for me, too," he said. "I'm heading back to my place to grab a few supplies. Then I'll be right back, and we'll both go find them. Okay?"

Liane stared up at him, her lips pressed together while she thought. When the tension in her shoulders eased, he took it as a sign of surrender.

"Go get what you need," she said.

He hurried home, then filled hiking canteens and grabbed the small survival kit he always kept stocked for his forays into the forest. With fire a possibility, his thoughts automatically turned to wildlife on the move, so he slipped a bear spray holster onto his belt just in case.

Stashing a few energy bars in the pouch, he quickly called Micah Fortney, a longtime hotshot firefighter. Getting no answer, Jake settled for leaving a detailed voice mail explaining where he was heading and why. It was probably for the best that Micah hadn't picked up, because he knew his old friend would give him holy hell for going out at night with a half-hysterical woman in tow. But nothing would convince Liane to stay at home while he rode out to find her family. She would only follow in his wake, giving him one more missing person to worry about.

A missing person he couldn't help but care for, no matter how clear she'd made it that she didn't want his company.

He grabbed a jacket against the chill that stole over the mountain nights even in late August, then shoved both his phone and a rechargeable two-way radio left over from his firefighting days into the pockets. After locking up the cabin, he made his way back to the corral…

…only to find that Liane had already gone, taking both the pinto mare and Misty.

Left behind just as he'd been, the river of horses continued milling restlessly, causing him to wonder whether the animals were still worked up over Liane's panic, or did they sense, as he did, that the worst was yet to come?

Liane knew Jake would be hurt that she had left him, but as she negotiated the easier portion of the lower trail, she couldn't allow herself to worry about the man who served as an unwelcome reminder of the worst decisions of her life. Still, an image blazed up before her of the stiff-necked pride written in his deep brown eyes and etched into his chiseled features. Wounded pride, when she'd brought up his injury.

Despite how often she'd seen him running lately, she couldn't imagine he was up to this night ride, no matter how brave and confident he'd sounded, how quick he'd been to take charge. But the more she tried to convince herself she was better off without him, the more she longed for someone, anyone, she could lean on, if only for tonight.

An image formed in her mind of another tall, strong man, this one standing over her to take aim…. A crack of thunder had her flinching with the memory, an old nightmare carved from shadow. A nightmare that served as another unwelcome reminder of the high price she'd paid for trusting the wrong man with the things most precious to her.

A thin branch slapped across her cheekbone, a stinging whiplash that had her hissing through her teeth and hauling back on the reins. The realization that she could easily have lost an eye brought home the point Jake had been trying to get through to her. She could end up hurt or even dead out here, with no chance of help for either herself or her family until morning.

A shaggy, four-legged form emerged from the under-growth ahead. Whining, Misty took a few steps forward, then circled back, as if encouraging Liane to hurry.

Liane nudged the pinto with her heels and followed the dog. A great favorite of the trail ride customers, the shepherd often accompanied her father on his trips, her long legs and incredible endurance allowing her to keep up with the horses. Even in the dark, the dog's experience and eagerness to see her beloved master would allow her to pick up the familiar trail.

Imagining their reunion, with Misty leaping up to lick Dad's face, then racing around Cody and Kenzie in happy circles, Liane managed to slow her breathing, to focus her thoughts as she'd been taught, on the most positive of out-comes rather than imagining all manner of disaster.

The technique seemed to be working, until another clap of thunder echoed off the rocks around her and she finally allowed herself to admit what she was smelling.

As the first faint wisps of wood smoke filtered among the trunks and understory bushes, the pinto pranced side-ways and nickered.

More worried than ever, Liane urged the mare for-ward. Time and time again the horse balked, and then the shepherd whined and circled back to find her. Perhaps the smoke was frightening the dog, too. Or maybe Misty was reacting to the same sixth sense that was warning Liane that her family was in more danger than ever. Either way, they all fed on each other's apprehension, with Misty's whining becoming more insistent and Liane digging her heels into the nervous pinto, pushing her forward ever faster. Far too fast, considering the darkness pressing in around her flashlight's bright beam, and the trail's grow-ing steepness and unevenness beneath the pinto's hooves.

An overhanging tree limb, not a stumble, knocked Liane from the saddle when she failed to duck in time to avoid it.

She landed with a painful grunt, the wind knocked out of her as first her body and then the back of her head slammed into the rocky ground. Her lungs suddenly empty and her ears ringing, she barely made out the sound of the mare's receding hooves. Racing back home, Liane thought miserably, to the safety of the herd.

Seconds later the air that had been knocked from her returned with a noisy gasp. With the influx of oxygen, pinpoints of light exploded in her vision, the only light, since the flashlight had been knocked from her hand and shattered.

By thinking of her family, she ignored her throbbing head and fought past the bleeding edge of terror. Horseless as she was, and injured as she might be, if she lost control now, she could die here. And whatever happened, she re-fused to let her family's hopes die with her.

"I can do this," she assured herself. "I *will* do it."

The familiar words triggered a memory, and she saw herself as if from above, lying beside the kicked-in door of that motel room in Las Vegas, her body painting a bloody swath on the cheap carpet as she dragged herself to the phone. An agonizing journey of eight feet had seemed more like eight miles, every inch fueled by the terror that Mac would come back any second, only this time she would be unable to keep him from the locked bathroom and the children.

Skin crawling, Liane told herself that if she could find the strength and courage to get through that night and the ordeal of the trial that followed—a trial that had been overshadowed in the press by the far more titillating case of a celebrity accused of groping showgirls—she could certainly make her way through this one. With no better option, she took stock of her situation, assessing her pain to figure out whether she was going to have to limp or even drag herself to find her family. Because find them she would, no matter what it cost her.

Misty reemerged from the smoky layer that hugged the ground like moon-touched mist. This time, though, the dog remained at Liane's side, her damp nose and little kisses urging her mistress to rise.

Pushing herself onto hands and knees, Liane struggled to stand, then cried out at the sharp pain that followed, and night's obsidian curtain crashed down on her, obliterating every conscious thought.

Chapter 2

At first, Jake took the sound for more thunder, but moments later he recognized the clatter of steel horseshoes on the rocky ground. Could Liane be coming back already?

The buckskin gelding he had borrowed lifted his head and neighed loudly. When the greeting was answered, Jake knew the animal ahead must be one of the buckskin's stable mates.

Pointing his flashlight down the trail ahead, he called, "Liane?"

His heart sank when the riderless pinto emerged from the dark.

Jake urged his mount forward, then leaned over to catch the mare's trailing reins. "Liane! Where are you?"

His words echoed through the woods, mingling with the thin smoke. Rather than the answer that he hoped for, the sky flashed white, and thunder shook the air. With the pinto squealing and struggling to escape, his own horse fought for his head, clearly planning to join the mare in a run for the safety of the stable.

His balance hampered by his prosthetic leg, Jake had a hell of a time convincing both animals that he, and not their flight instinct, was in charge. Though he was far from an expert horseman, he'd watched Deke on enough occasions to mimic the soothing, confident tones that normally put horses at ease.

But he was no Deke Mason, and there was nothing normal about tonight. Jake might have succeeded in keeping both animals from bolting, but he wasn't kidding himself. The buckskin would dump him and race the pinto back home if he let his guard down for a moment.

Still, he risked calling out again, "Liane, can you hear me?"

Once again there was no answer other than the echo of his own words.

Jake swore, then swallowed past the lump in his throat. In spite of her coolness and the fact that she'd once more wasted no time ditching him, his gut clenched as he imagined finding her out here somewhere, hurt, her braid unraveled and her delicate face—a face he remembered kissing so thoroughly on that last day, before she'd gone off to college—transformed into a mask of blood. Just as painful as the idea of losing the first girl, the *only* one, he'd ever offered his love was the idea of telling Cody and Kenzie that their mother had been killed in an attempt to find them.

That, just as he had been, they would have to be raised by their only surviving relative, a single grandparent.

Breathing a silent prayer that it wouldn't come to that, he continued forward, grateful that the surefooted buckskin, at least, seemed to have recovered his senses. Feeling a little more secure, he pulled the radio from his pocket and switched it to the channel he knew the Masons used.

"Deke?" he said into it. "This is Jake Whittaker. What's your location? Is Liane there with you?"

Again and again he tried to raise the older man as static crackled, coinciding with the flickering lightning. Recalling how he'd seen Deke tinkering with his handheld only a few days earlier, Jake nearly gave up hope before he heard the indistinct chatter of an excited male voice, but the transmission was so broken up, he couldn't make out a single word.

Though Misty would ordinarily growl at a stranger's approach, she fanned her bushy tail as a rider emerged from the darkness. Blinded by the powerful flashlight beam cutting through the smoky haze, Liane raised her arm to shield her eyes and called, "Who is it?"

A horse whinnied as it was reined to an abrupt stop, while behind it, a second animal danced and snorted.

"Thank God," came Jake's voice. "When I found your horse running loose, I was afraid you might be—are you hurt? I'd get down, but..."

She nodded, knowing that he would find it tough to climb back on board a nervous horse without a mounting block. "I fell and bumped my head. Smashed my flashlight, too, but I'll be okay. And I'm really sorry I ran off the way I did." Her words were clipped, embarrassed, reminding her of another time when she'd left him, but she couldn't afford to waste time thinking of things she could never undo. Overhead, lightning flashed, a long, low growl of thunder on its heels. "I've been out of my mind worrying, but at least the fall knocked a little sense into me."

"I'm worried about this smoke. This lightning's definitely sparked off something."

"Do you have any idea where the fire is?" She prayed he wouldn't say Elk Creek Canyon.

"Can't see anything from this far down the mountain," he said. "Smoke could be blowing in from miles away or over the next ridge. Considering the weather, more than likely there are multiple ignition points."

Anxiety knotted her stomach. If there was fire between her and her family, then what? The only other way into the canyon was an even rougher path off an old logging road so far to the north they would have to ride back home, then trailer the horses to reach it.

"You think you can make it back up on your horse again?" Jake asked.

Swallowing hard, she nodded. "If you can hold her still." She limped over to the mare. "It's all right, Queen. It's okay, sweetie," she crooned, until the horse accepted her presence. Before remounting, she forced herself to take time to stroke the silken neck, keeping her voice soft yet assured, and her hands gentle and steady. Earlier she'd allowed herself to get so worked up that she'd forgotten everything she knew about working with horses, and it had cost her dearly. She couldn't afford to make the same mistake again.

Feeling the mare relax beneath her touch, she reached up, grabbing the saddle horn and cantle, then swung aboard in one swift, sure motion. Though the movement had her head spinning again, she swallowed back a groan and leaned over the horn, imagining herself a rock in one of Yosemite's wildest rivers, a stationary object that pain and panic flowed past.

Jake leaned close to hand her the reins. "You're hurting, Liane, and a head injury's nothing to fool with. We need to get you back home."

Straightening, she forced herself to ignore the worry in his voice. "Listen, Jake, I'm really glad you're here. But if you came all this way just to tell me to turn around, you're wasting your breath."

"Wouldn't be the first time," he reminded her. "But it's not safe here—"

"Which means my family's in danger."

"Which means," he insisted, "that your dad's more than likely found someplace to take shelter with the kids. Someplace off the trail, where we could ride right past him."

"I know every cave and overhang, all the spots he uses when a sudden storm comes up. I'll find them, Jake, I know it. And after I finish hugging them all within an inch of their lives, I swear I'll never let them out of my sight again."

A gust of wind had the trees swaying, their scraping, rattling branches making crazy shadows as heat lightning strobe-lit the dark sky.

"It's getting worse," Jake said. "There's no way your father would want you out in this."

The urgency in his tone had her on alert. "Is there something you aren't telling me? Something you've found out?"

"I haven't been able to reach anybody—too much static. But I don't like this wind. It gets high enough, it'll bring down a lot of this dry timber and feed the fires."

"We're wasting time here. Let's get moving." As she spoke, she heard her voice going cold and felt herself stiffening, the way she always did around him since her return. Because she'd understood almost from the day she'd moved back to her dad's house last year that Jake Whittaker was more than an uncomfortable reminder of the past. He was a danger to her, with his handsome face and hard, masculine body, a body so defined and sculpted that the briefest glimpse of him in a tight T-shirt was enough to weaken her knees. And enough to rekindle a memory so bittersweet, it tasted of her own tears.

But there was more, far more than a body born to tempt her, from his willingness to help her dad out at a moment's notice to the way the two of them would get to grinning—though that deep, open laugh that she remembered had been another of the casualties of last summer's fire. Jake was so good-natured around her kids, too, happily putting up with Cody's tendency to talk the ears off anyone who would listen and gently teasing smiles out of her shy daughter. Seeing them together reminded her all too painfully of how often he'd daydreamed aloud of someday having a big family of his own to make up for losing his own parents at a young age.

She'd known instinctively that he was the sort of man who could entice her to forget the years that lay between them, the sort of man who could sneak back into her heart if she didn't pay attention. But she could never risk forgetting how the man she'd eventually gone on to marry had seemed every bit as kind, as strong, as stable, until, seemingly overnight, he'd changed. Mac was never convicted of embezzling a fortune from the securities firm where he'd been working, but the shame of the public allegation had changed him into a violent, paranoid monster overnight. The sort of monster she could never risk allowing into her life or her bed—much less her children's lives—again.

"You're sure you're okay to ride?" Jake asked, his concern so at odds with her memories of her ex that guilt lashed her.

"I am," she said, feeling even worse as she recalled the way she'd implied earlier that he would only hold her back. Despite that, he'd come to find her. "And thank you. Thanks for riding out."

Taking the lead, he nudged his mount into a jog and said over his shoulder, "It's no problem."

As she clucked at the pinto to get her trotting, discomfort lit up Liane's bruised nerve endings like a switch-board. But she kept her mouth shut, not wanting to give Jake another excuse to argue that they should turn around.

Besides, he must be hurting, too, considering that he hadn't been back on a horse since last summer's fires, and she didn't hear him complaining.

She made a mental note to bake him some more of those gooey caramel brownies he was so crazy about once this was all over—neighborly offerings that were far easier for her than conversation. Or maybe she would even invite him over for dinner one night, the way her father and the kids all kept suggesting.

Because she had the strength to manage that and keep her distance. The strength and, most of all, the experience to remind her of just how deceptive, how deadly dangerous, a handsome, helpful, seemingly safe man could prove to be.

Sheriff Harry Wallace reluctantly admitted to himself that he was getting too damned old for nights like this one. With the sky crackling and the wind howling, his office phones were ringing off the hook, and the few deputies who had survived the most recent round of budget cuts were scattered from hell to breakfast, checking out "smell of smoke" and automatic alarm calls from systems tripped off by power surges. To make matters worse, his heartburn was killing him, probably because he'd been drinking coffee by the pot-full in an effort to stay focused.

He was trying to shovel down another bite from the warmed-and-rewarmed dinner that his sister had dropped by when his hapless young assistant came fluttering through the door, a paper clutched in her hand. Seeing the terrified look on her freckled face, he put down his fork and snapped, "What is it now, Camille?"

Her flush deepened, making him feel guilty. It was his fault, not hers, for hiring some fool kid right out of high school to replace the office manager who'd kept this place running like a top for decades. On nights like this one, he wished he had retired with Gladys rather than settle for the sort of help he could hire for only a whisker above minimum wage. The sort of help he'd had to shake his own damned family tree to find.

"I— I'm so sorry, Sheriff Wallace," his sister's granddaughter managed. "I hate to bother you, but—but somehow this fax must've slipped behind the cabinet. I just found it, but it's marked Urgent, so I—"

"Well, give it here," he said, reaching out to snatch the paper from her. He almost choked on his casserole when he peered through his reading glasses at the header.

The Nevada Department of Corrections

Victim Services Unit

VICTIM NOTIFICATION REQUEST: Urgent

Dated three days earlier, it went on to name Liane Mason, giving her father's address along with the handwritten notation: *Please remind victim to update her phone number for our system!*

But it was the message that followed that had Wallace pushing away from his desk and getting to his feet. "Damn it, Camille. I told Liane Mason not to worry. Told her that Deke and her kids would be just fine 'til morning. And we were sitting on something like this?"

Camille shrank back, her green eyes streaming. "I'm really sorry, Uncle Harry," she said, forgetting her promise not to call him that here at the office.

He held up one hand for silence, grabbing his desk phone with the other. On his call log, he found Liane Mason's number and pressed the buttons, his mind worrying over how to break the news. While it was still possible—

he would even call it likely—that the late return of his old-est friend Deke Mason and Deke's grandkids had nothing to do with a prison break over in Nevada, he knew Liane wouldn't buy it for a second. Already scared out of her wits, there was no telling what she might do.

"Hell's bells. Call's not connecting," he grumbled. "What do you want to bet this wind's knocked a tree across the phone lines?"

"Is there something I can do to help?" Camille pleaded.

He nodded, grabbing his hat and jacket from the coat rack in the corner. "Yeah, there is. You can dump my din-ner in the trash and hold down the fort. If anybody needs me, I'm heading over to the Masons' place to check on Liane. I'll call from there to let you know what's going on."

With one foot out the door, he paused and darted a look back at his red-faced grandniece. "And one more thing, Camille. Quit wasting your time crying and start praying for the Mason family instead."

Jake's gut tightened with the nagging suspicion that he was making a mistake not snatching the reins from Liane and forcing her to turn back. As worried as he was about her family, he'd known Deke Mason long enough to feel confident that, as long as he still drew breath, the expe-rienced outdoorsman would see to his grandkids' safety.

He tried to picture his friend sitting cross-legged on a cave floor, regaling his grandchildren with story after story as they snuggled under the old blankets he had cached there for just such an emergency. Knowing Deke, the old man had them convinced that their extended trip, from the broken radio to the storm itself, was all part of some grand adventure.

And if any living creature threatened—whether it was an agitated bear, a rabid coyote or one of the rattlesnakes common to the area—Deke would pull out the .50 caliber revolver he always carried on trips and take care of the situation. He would probably be mad enough to shoot Jake, too, if he let anything happen to Liane.

They continued pressing forward, making better time as the storm diminished. The horses' steel shoes rang against stone and the leather of their saddles creaked. The air, too, became clearer as the wind shifted direction

"See, this isn't so bad," she called to him. "Maybe the weather people got it wrong and the worst is past already."

"I hope so," he said.

But the respite didn't last much longer before a new storm rolled in, the dry wind rising until showers of golden-brown pine needles rained down on their heads. With no other warning, lightning forked across the sky, followed by the distinctive smell of ozone and a boom that shook the air.

At the crash, both horses started, and Jake had to shift his weight abruptly to stay seated.

"You all right?" Liane called, even as her own mount danced and snorted, tossing her head nervously.

"I'll be fine," he said, though the healed fracture in his back ached, jarred by the sudden movement. The leg throbbed, too, the phantom pain of severed nerves sending false reminders of the shattering injury. But during his years of wilderness firefighting, Jake had learned to shove his physical discomfort to a locked compartment of his brain where it could be dealt with sometime later. "I don't know how much more of this these horses will put up with, though."

As the wind gusted, there was another loud crack, and a large branch hurtled down only steps away. This time the buckskin dropped his head and kicked up, his body twisting with such sudden force that Jake went flying from the saddle.

He landed facedown with a grunt, the shock of the impact rattling every bone and filling. Before he could react, Liane was kneeling beside him, and the dog was in his face, whining and licking at his forehead.

"Jake, are you all right?" she asked. "Out of the way, Misty."

Pushing himself up on his elbows, he registered the concern in her words—along with the clatter of both their horses' hoof beats, receding down the trail.

"I'm in one piece, I think," he said, reaching for his leg to confirm it. Finding the prosthesis still in place, he added, "But I'm sorry about losing the horses."

"Not your fault—I should've known to hold on to my reins, but when I saw you lying down there…" She raised her voice to be heard above the wind as the shepherd paced around her nervously. "Here, let me help you up."

Under other circumstances, he might have bristled at the offer, but tonight he was grateful to use her for balance. Accepting the hand she offered, he pushed himself upright and held his breath until he was certain he could stand unassisted.

Another bolt of lightning lit the sky, and thunder crashed even closer.

"We can't keep going in this weather—or risk going back, either!" he shouted. "We need to find one of those caves or overhangs you mentioned before we get fried— or killed by a falling tree."

Mingled with the smell of smoke, the piney tang of fresh-cut evergreens filled the air around them—an all-too-sharp reminder of the tree that had struck him last year.

"You're right." She stooped to pick up his high-impact

flashlight where it had fallen, its beam still shining brightly. "But are you sure you're up for the hike?"

"If you can do it, I can," he vowed, despite his aching body.

Nodding, she linked her arm through his and started walking, both of them bent low against the smoke-laced wind.

Chapter 3

The climb to the closest of the caves Liane remembered would have been daunting for an able-bodied hiker on a sunny day. With tonight's wind and darkness, it was a nightmare, but Jake kept up with her far better than she would have expected, even managing to hold her upright when she slid on loose rock.

As they made their way upslope, she soon found herself gasping with exertion. Spent, she stopped to rest, and fresh doubt crept into her mind.

"Jake," she said, "I'm not—I'm not so sure about this anymore. I thought I knew the way, but—"

He found her hand and took it. "Take a moment. Get your bearings."

Even now, with the wind whipping and the thunder echoing around them, there was something calming in his voice, something that steadied her, just as her mare had responded to her touch.

"I'm pretty sure you're right, if that helps," he said. "I remember the cave. It's the one you took me to that time."

She shook her head, her face heating. "No, not that place. It's—that was such a long time ago. I don't even remember where that was, exactly."

But of course she *did*. She would never forget untying the rolled blanket from behind her saddle, would never forget leading the boyfriend she'd been so certain she would be with forever by the hand and...

She remembered every moment of it in such vivid detail that she was relieved it was too far to walk to in these conditions, even though, for all she knew, her dad might still stash emergency food, water and raingear there the way he once had. She told herself she couldn't allow her focus to get mired in the past, not with her family out here somewhere, under this same unsettled sky.

"You were right before," she said, raising her voice to be heard above the rush of wind. "Everything looks so different in the dark."

Even the man she'd been avoiding all these months.

As his flashlight's beam caught a distinctive, chair-shaped rock, she murmured, "This is right, yes," and started uphill again, this time moving so quickly that he had to struggle to keep pace.

But all too soon she froze, hearing a new sound from a higher elevation—the splintering crash of a tree falling, then spearing its way downhill, its branches snagging and snapping as it picked up speed and sent rocks plummeting.

"Run, Jake! Hurry!" she cried, adrenaline slamming through her system. "Avalanche!"

Sure enough, Sheriff Harry Wallace found the lines down in not just one but three places along rural Black Oak Road, where trees had fallen across the power and phone wires, effectively cutting off the Mason ranch and a scattering of vacation cabins. The road, too, was obstructed, but he was able to get around or over everything that stood in his way, thanks to four-wheel-drive.

When he reached the homestead, he didn't see so much as a candle burning or hear the generator running, though he found a silver Jeep he recognized as Liane's parked next to Deke's truck. A sinking feeling in his gut, Harry took his flashlight and checked out the perimeter, with a pause to knock at both the front and back doors and call out Liane's name.

No answer, but there were no signs of forced entry, either, and he could see the red lights of the house's alarm system—which evidently had a battery backup—blinking, showing that it had been armed. All signs, Harry suspected, that the terrified young mother had done exactly as she'd threatened and ridden off to find her family.

On a night like this one, with her thieving, murderous ex-husband on the loose. The same man, if one could call him that, who had stalked and shot her two years back.

As Harry passed the former hotshot's pickup on the way to the old bunkhouse, he laid a hand on the older Ford's blue hood. Cool, as he'd expected, since Whittaker rarely left the place after last summer's fateful fire. Punishing himself, people were saying, though the investigation that followed had cleared him of all fault in the deaths of the men working under him.

Like most people he knew, Harry thought highly of Jake, but he understood the younger man's decision to move away from town. Harry had felt guilty enough after being forced to lay off four deputies. How much more painful must it be for Jake, knowing that they'd died following his orders—and that a handful of the dead men's family members had openly, aggressively, questioned the decisions he had made that terrible night?

Taking in the darkened windows, Harry stepped onto the cabin's front porch. "Jake?" he called.

No answer. But when he tapped at the door, it swung inward with a loud creak. "What the hell?" he murmured as his flashlight's beam raked the interior.

The place had been ransacked, the mattress and two upholstered chairs shredded, and the contents of every drawer strewn across the floor. But this had been no robbery, because a laptop computer lay among the mess with its screen smashed, along with a television and what looked to have been an expensive stereo system.

Alarm punching at his chest, he went inside, dreading the thought that he might come across Whittaker's body buried in the wreckage. Grateful to find no sign of either Jake or any blood as he checked the small bathroom and the bedroom space behind a low partition, Harry struggled to come up with a theory to make sense of the destruction. Could McCleary have come back here and grown jealous of the handsome former boyfriend living too close to his ex for comfort? Or maybe this vandalism had another source. Perhaps someone was still holding a grudge against Jake for what had happened last summer. Or, who knew, maybe it had been some local kids on a drunken spree, or even a hungry bear that had found the door ajar and wandered inside. As for why Jake wasn't there… Knowing the man's keen sense of responsibility would trump whatever hurt feelings he might harbor over some old high school romance gone wrong, Harry could easily imagine him riding out with Liane to keep her from searching for her family alone.

As Harry hurried back toward his SUV, he suspected he was deluding himself to even consider that this break-in was coincidental. Still, he prayed it was possible that Jake and all the Masons would somehow get back home safely. Foolish as it might be, he couldn't help hoping his earlier wishful thinking would prove true, and his old friend's delay in returning with his grandchildren would prove to be no more criminal than a broken radio and a horse with colic or a thrown shoe.

And above all, he prayed it would have nothing to do with his own failure to warn Deke and Liane that this might happen.

Passing the corral on his way back to his vehicle, Harry went still at the sound of whinnying, then slowly turned his flashlight on the horses.

A dozen or so had crowded near the far end of the enclosure, their attention on another animal shambling into view. As Harry approached, he saw the white foam of exertion on the sweat-soaked chestnut hide, along with a grayish coating of dust.

No, not dust, he realized, his breath hitching as he registered the acrid odor. Ash—and the horse's tail was singed, the long, brown hairs all crisped or missing. Which had to mean that there was fire between here and Elk Creek Canyon.

"Where the hell are you, Deke?" he murmured, more worried than ever.

Then his gaze found the saddle, and his stomach lurched as he took in the stirrups, which had been shortened for a child's legs. Even worse, he saw dark splotches marring the brown leather.

Bloodstains, he was certain, and so large they indicated a serious, if not mortal, wound.

"God forgive me," he murmured, raising his light at the sound of approaching hoof beats. A cloud of dust preceded Deke's big black mule, Waco, as it came hobbling from the brush. Like the horse, the mule was saddled, but Waco's tack included a special holster Deke had had made to fit over the pommel.

Deke's revolver remained in place, the sight of it adding to the nausea swirling in the sheriff's stomach.

After letting both exhausted animals into the corral, he used a handkerchief to pull the weapon from its holster. A sniff of the muzzle and a check of the chambers confirmed that whatever had happened, his old friend had never even gotten off a shot.

But he wouldn't give up hope. He couldn't, so Harry broke into a run, heading back toward his Yukon and his radio, a radio he would use to call in backup from the state, the hotshot fire crews, the search and rescue teams—whoever the hell he could think of—to save whichever of the Masons might still survive.

Sizing up the crashing sounds from above in a split second, Jake grabbed Liane, holding her firmly in spite of her struggle to run from the avalanche.

"We're okay here," he shouted as the slide rocketed past, smashing down more trees with an earsplitting racket that far outstripped the thunder.

She held on to him for dear life, her nails digging into his back. Within seconds it was over, leaving her breathing hard.

"There, you see?" He was breathing just as hard as he gave her a squeeze before releasing her. "But we'd better get out of here before the next one comes."

"I can't—can't believe we're still alive," she said.

His senses heightened by their near miss, he grew hyperaware of the warmth of her breath against his face, the way her stiffness slowly dissolved into trembling. The sweet familiarity of her body pressed against his surged through his veins, along with the pell-mell thumping of her heart against his chest.

On more than one occasion he'd dreamed of holding her this close again, a fantasy crafted from stolen glimpses of a woman who treated him as if he were some stranger. A woman whom Deke Mason had warned him needed space.

Jake stepped back from her, heat rushing to his face. A man, especially a man who'd been without female companionship for as many months as he had, couldn't be blamed for what ran through his head on dark nights in his chilly cabin, especially not with the first woman he'd ever been with living so close by. But Liane was terrified, and with good reason. His own heart was still pounding with the adrenaline surging through his bloodstream. "It's over now. You're all right."

"We're safe?"

"For the moment, anyway, but we'd better get to shelter before it happens again."

She nodded, then disentangled herself and started moving back up the mountain. Minutes later she crouched under the lip of a low overhang and waved him inside.

"Whoa, there," he warned, stepping past her with the flashlight. "Better let me check first, just to make sure nothing else has holed up in here. We definitely don't want to end up getting between a trapped animal and freedom."

He ducked his head inside and used his light to skim the recesses of a cave only marginally larger than a box stall. Relieved not to spot any glowing eyes, he said, "Looks clear, but watch where you step. Snakes can be hard to see."

"I'll take my chances with the snakes," she said. "I just want out of this wind."

She sounded so exhausted that he instinctively—foolishly, he warned himself—reached for her. To his relief, she didn't fight, only laid her head on his shoulder and gradually relaxed into his embrace. Despite the circumstances, he liked the way she fit—and felt—against him all too well.

The moment served as another painful reminder of how good they'd been together once, and how isolated he'd been since leaving the rehabilitation center. When was the last time he had touched anyone for more than a brief handshake? But with the grandmother who had raised him long gone and his former fellow firefighters too sharp a reminder of things he could never change, he'd told himself that he was better off focusing on adapting to his new life than pining for the old one.

Maybe he'd told himself wrong, at least the part about living like some kind of recluse. Maybe he should adopt a big, slobbery dog that he could run and roughhouse with, and spoil rotten when no one else was looking. Having something he could claim might keep him from latching on to a woman who didn't want him and a family that wasn't his.

Or better yet, maybe he just needed to remember the sleepless nights and crushing pain she'd cost him at eighteen, then get out there and find himself a woman with a heart. A woman who would give him a family of his own.

"Tell me, Jake," she said, the hollowness in her voice making him feel guilty for judging her so harshly. "Tell me this is just some awful nightmare. Tell me we're both sleeping, and Dad and the kids are safe at home."

"I wish I could do that," he said honestly, "or snap my fingers and make everything right for you. But until this storm dies down, there's nothing I can do."

"We could call for help, at least."

"I'll try," he promised. "But let's get you out of this wind first. You're dead on your feet."

Unwinding his arms from around her, he edged a little

farther inside. Outside, the wind shifted, setting off an unearthly howl as it gusted across the cave mouth like a child blowing over the top of a bottle.

He focused his flashlight on a corner where leaf litter had accumulated and kicked at it with his prosthetic foot, but nothing stirred or slithered.

"Why don't you sit here and rest?" he suggested, his voice echoing in the enclosed space. "I'll try the radio again."

He'd turned and made it several steps away when she said, "Thanks, Jake. And…I'm sorry."

"Sorry for what?" he asked, wondering if it was possible that she, too, might be thinking of their past. That she might be regretting the way things had ended.

"For dragging you into this. And for the way…" as she knelt down in the dry leaves, the noise drowned out her next few words "…probably think I'm the biggest bitch in the county, the way I've acted toward you since I came back."

"What way's that?" he asked, playing the Clueless Male card. Pretending that it hadn't cut him to the bone.

"Never mind," she said, fending off Misty's attempt to lick her cheek. "I just want you to know how much I appreciate what you're doing for me. Especially since—"

"Not just for you," he interrupted, doing his best to compete with the gale. "Your dad's been—he's a great guy. A great man. When I first brought up the idea of fixing up the old bunkhouse in exchange for cheaper rent, I was only looking to save some money toward a new truck. I never banked on him insisting on lending me a hand—or turning into one of the best friends I've ever had."

A lump formed in his throat, but there was no way he was admitting that in truth Deke felt like a father to him— the father he'd never had, since his real dad had turned his back on the family when he was too young to remember the selfish SOB, or mourn him when he'd died a few years later. Jake might know wilderness firefighting, but he didn't know much about construction. It was Deke who'd steered him away from a guest cabin whose mushy floorboards belied a weak foundation, Deke who'd taught him that when it came to a home, a business or a family, a rock-solid footing was the only place a man could put his trust.

"And I never really thought I liked kids that much," he went on, remembering how the idea that Liane had had children with another man—children that might have been his—had stung, "but Cody cracks me up with all his stories, and Kenzie's the cutest little thing. She looks just like you, you know. It's the eyes."

"I keep telling them they shouldn't bother you so much." Her voice shook with emotion. "I know you need peace and quiet for your work."

"They don't bother—well, yeah, they do sometimes," he said, thinking of times when he'd been in the midst of some complex, tedious translation and one or the other of them rapped at his door, then raced away to hide around the corner, their giggles giving them away each time. Though his deadlines were often tight, he sometimes took a break on the porch and shared some of the caramel brownies they always seemed to know their mother had sent over. "To tell you the truth, if they ever really did quit bugging me, I'd miss the hell out of them."

As the shaggy gray dog curled up beside her, Jake looked away, embarrassed by the surge of affection he felt for her family—and the lengths to which he would be willing to go to reunite them. Because they loved each other, their bond forming a closed circle he couldn't help but want to protect, even though he stood on the outside.

Clearing his throat, he pulled out the radio and raised it. "Be right back."

Between the howling of the wind and the crackling of lightning, he knew his odds of getting a message through on the handheld were slim. Still, he tried repeatedly, attempting to time his calls for Deke Mason and his requests for assistance between the flashes and the interference they created.

As the storm diminished for the moment, he once again heard a male voice intermittently breaking through the static. Though Jake didn't recognize the speaker, he couldn't miss the panic in his clipped words. Listening carefully, he made out something about a pair of hikers in distress and being boxed in by flames....

The image took him back to the night his own men had become trapped while following his orders. The night when the blaze had abruptly shifted and raced the wrong way, running downhill and against the wind, in defiance of the known laws of fire behavior.

Memory spiraled in on him, followed by the shock and horror he'd felt hearing their calls on the radio, the panicked need to get to them and lead them out to safety.

His rational mind had known it had been already too late, that there had been no way he could have made it in time and nothing he could have done if he'd gotten there except die by their sides. Still, he'd grabbed Micah and raced straight for them, the truck jouncing over the rutted track until it bottomed out and could go no farther. Though Micah had fought to stop him, Jake had leaped out from behind the wheel, running through the black smoke.

With a tortured crack, a huge trunk had given way an instant before he'd felt a shattering blow followed by utter blackness. And worst of all, the accident hadn't made a bit of difference to the three men who had burned to death a mile away while Micah saved him from the same fate.

"Hikers, what is your location?" Jake asked now, his voice shaking with his need to have things end differently this time around. But no matter how many times he repeated his transmission, it was clear the speaker couldn't hear him.

The hikers were cut off from help. And with no way to contact the authorities or guide them to a place of safety, he could only listen helplessly until the increasingly frantic calls gave way to silence.

A silence overwhelmed by static and the howling of the storm.

Chapter 4

If the gushing wind and crashing thunder didn't do it, Mac was certain that Smash and Goose—and maybe even AK, who'd decided to meet up with them later because of his leg injury—meant to kill him. From the very start, he could now see, they had planned to off him the minute he found the cash, then split his share among themselves.

Only now they meant to force him to kill the witnesses—his children—first, though Smash swore they only meant to use the kids as leverage.

Could that be right? Or was it just another lie, like all the others? Mac could barely think straight, the images of those two babies flashing through his brain like lightning.

They weren't babies anymore, he knew. In fact, he doubted he would be able to pick them out on a crowded playground, despite the brief glimpse he'd gotten when they had disappeared into the woods. But the brown-eyed boy, at least, was his for certain—his only sure legacy in the world, though he'd never been much of a father to him.

But it wasn't his fault at all. It had been the medication. He understood that now. The pills were so easy to get and supposedly so harmless that doctors prescribed them to schoolkids by the millions. He'd only meant to use a few to sharpen his attention to detail, to give him an edge against the younger competitors always snapping at his heels, so he could take care of his growing family. At first the drug had worked, but then the young hounds had upped their game, too, so he'd started snorting coke, until his thoughts had raced round and round his mind like those little electric cars he'd had as a boy, the ones that could only go so fast before they flew right off their cheap plastic racetrack. But no matter how he'd fought it, one idea had clung stubbornly: the suspicion that Liane had been plotting his destruction so she could run back to the man her father, that old SOB, had come right out and told him to his face that his daughter should've married.

Mac could still picture the way Deke Mason had looked right through him that day as if all his accomplishments, all the money he had made by his own wits, had meant not a damned thing. As if an old man who always smelled of leather, sweat and horseshit had any right to judge the way he treated his own wife.

Fresh resentment boiled up with the certainty that Liane's father had backed him into this corner. The way Mac saw it, the old man had forced his hand this afternoon just to make him look bad.

But as long as Mac was still a man, he had choices. Especially when it came to the two kids who bore his name.

"You told us you knew these woods," Smash shouted above the wind, still angry that they'd lost the panicked horses. "So you'd damned well better find those brats fast, before Goose and me decide to cut our losses."

Just in case he'd missed the point, Goose came up and

grabbed him from behind, laying the cold steel of his knife against Mac's pulsing throat.

"Liane."

The voice woke her with a start, her body jerking so hard in response that her head banged against something as cold and unyielding as rock. No, it *was* rock. And the room was black, without the soft, safe glow of the alarm clock.

Because it wasn't a room, and she wasn't in her bed at home. She was back with *him,* subject to his insane demands, his violent temper. Her heart kicking into high gear, she swallowed back a cry. When a strangled whimper slipped out, she braced herself for whatever would come next.

"Storm's over." The words were quiet. "I thought you'd want to know."

Not Mac. *Not Mac. Not Mac...* He didn't have her, wasn't here.

With that realization her brain slipped back into gear, and awareness struck her like a landslide, bringing the memory of where she was—and why.

No less terrifying than the past, the present chilled her to the marrow. She dragged in a breath of air, thick and tainted with the bitterness of ash.

"Liane?" Jake asked softly. "Are you all right?"

A spasm of coughing gripped her, making it impossible to answer. When he switched on his flashlight, she blinked at the sudden brilliance, then focused on his gaze, the dark eyes that had once upon a time made her feel so safe. *Thank God.*

She nodded. "How long have I been sleeping?"

"A few hours, but don't worry. I've been awake. Listening to the weather and trying the radio from time to time."

Misty stretched and yawned beside her, fanning her

tail hopefully. Ignoring the dog, Liane asked, "Did you reach him?"

He shook his head. "Sorry, no, but I did pick up a distress call. Two backpackers, trapped by fire. They were panicking, disoriented, said they'd started off on the trailhead back at Smuggler's Gulch."

"That's a good distance from here." She wondered by what trick of the airwaves their words could have made it this far.

"After a while they stopped transmitting."

"Who was it? Did you get a name?"

"No name, and I have no idea. I only wish there was something, anything, I could've done."

Hearing his haunted tone, she asked, "Then you think they're...?"

"Dead? Probably. And I can't even contact search and rescue to send them for the bodies."

She began to tremble, imagining her own family ringed by flame, her children crying for her. Imagining that her best efforts, even with Jake's help, wouldn't be enough. Closing her eyes, she struggled to force back the images. But their terrified voices echoed through her mind. Her children's voices, ringing through a hostile wilderness.

"We don't know there's fire in Elk Creek Canyon," Jake said, giving her hand a lingering squeeze. "But we're nearly to the ridge already. We need to climb up above the tree line and see what we're dealing with."

"Sounds like a good idea." She coughed again, the sound raspy.

He pulled out a canteen. "Most of my water was on the horse, but here, have some of this."

"Thanks." Grateful for his generosity, she drank sparingly, just enough to calm her burning throat. Handing the canteen back, she admitted, "I had everything in my saddlebags. Everything except my stupid cell phone, for all the good it does us."

Pulling it out, she checked the time. "It's a little after 4:00 a.m. Sunrise comes at…what would you say, this time of year? Five? Five-thirty?"

"Sun might not make much difference, depending on the smoke."

"Then we may as well get moving."

Jake led the way back into the smoky darkness, moving toward the rocky spine that overlooked Elk Creek Canyon.

Liane stared past him, a lump tightening her throat. "Kenzie will need her inhaler. This bad air's going to play hell with her asthma."

"Your dad's got her medication, right?"

She nodded. "If he—yes, he has it."

"Then he'll take care of her," Jake assured her.

As they continued walking, she held on to the certainty in his voice, using it to tamp out the embers of panic whenever they threatened to ignite. For two years, even after her ex-husband's arrest and conviction, she had taken medication to help her with anxiety. Since coming home, she'd quietly weaned herself off the pills, preferring to rely on long walks and focused breathing to keep her fear in check, training that stood her in good stead now.

She tried to concentrate on the quiet rhythm of their footsteps, on the ebb and flow of oxygen as she filled and emptied her lungs. Still, her eyes pooled with tears, anxiety gnawing at her ability to function.

After they'd been hiking uphill for a few minutes, he pulled something from his pocket and tore into its wrapper. "Here, try one of these. They're not greatest tasting, but they'll give you energy."

"I'm not hungry." Terrified of what they might see

when they looked down into the canyon, she couldn't think of food.

"You need to eat." He pushed one into her hand. "Whether we end up hiking back out or moving forward, we'll be burning tons of calories. And I'm in no mood to carry you when your blood sugar crashes."

She sighed but didn't argue. "Here I thought you fire-fighters lived for that sort of thing."

"And here I thought you'd lost your sense of humor," he said dryly.

She forced herself to smile. "Just goes to show how little you really know me. The grown-up me, I mean."

Dutifully, she bit off a hunk of the energy bar. It tasted a little like honeyed, freeze-dried sawdust, but she forced herself to keep chewing anyway.

"I might get the chance to know you better," Jake told her, "if you wouldn't run for the house every time you catch sight of me."

"I don't run from you."

"Come on, Liane. You want to kid yourself? Fine, but I'm not buying it for a minute. After the hundredth time, it gets to be painfully obvious that a person's pretending not to see you and then scurrying for cover."

"I wave back when you wave at me." She hated how defensive she sounded, but she kept remembering the long hours they'd once spent talking about their dreams and ambitions…and how every one of his had revolved around creating the family he lacked. As a teenager with plans of her own, his intensity had scared her. Considering all she'd been through, the memory of that intensity had frightened her even more when she'd come home. "And I know we've spoken."

"When you absolutely can't avoid it."

"I've sent cookies, brownies, even pies, and cards from the children while you were still in rehab."

"And I've appreciated all of them. But I can't help wondering, why is it I have to resort to leaving thank-you notes when we live less than a hundred yards apart?"

"I—I'm a busy person. I work full-time, have two kids—"

"Never mind," he told her. "You don't have to make excuses. I just wanted to see if I could figure out if there was something I'd said or done to—"

"Not lately," she blurted, hating the reminder of her very worst decisions, along with everything that her mistakes had cost her. But even so, those same choices had given her the children she treasured, children whose existence was worth any price.

"What?" he asked. "Come on, Liane. Just tell me. Tell me what I've done to—"

"You're imagining things," she insisted, wincing at her own curtness. But better he should think her rude than force her to explain the memories triggered by his size, his build and that deep, masculine voice that scared her even though he, like those thankfully few male hotel guests who elicited the same reaction, had never done a thing to warrant her fear, not even for a moment. She hated feeling like a frightened mouse instead of the calm, competent professional she usually managed to portray at work, but she had no idea what to do other than avoid what the counselor called her "trigger points."

Someone should have told that to her father before he'd gone and invited Jake, the man he'd always thought she should have married, to move in. A good man of her own age, a local man who would never hurt her. An inescapable reminder that, even at thirty, she couldn't yet be trusted to make her own choices. Worried as she was about her father, that slap in the face still made her furious.

Her appetite gone, she fed the last half of the energy bar to Misty when Jake wasn't looking.

He grew quiet as he moved from one flattened boulder to the next, focusing on his footing to scale a natural formation that looked almost like a staircase built by giants. The elevation had her breathing so hard that she still managed to fall behind, despite his cautious progress.

He had pulled substantially ahead when a smaller rock shifted beneath his prosthetic foot. He lost his balance, then cursed as he went down on hands and knees.

"You okay there?" she asked.

But he was staring to his left, through a gap between the squared shoulders of two huge rocks. "Wait!" he warned sharply. "Don't come any closer."

"What is it?" she asked, unable to see from where she was.

Misty bounded up the rocks to reach Jake. At first the dog tried to lick him, evidently considering it her duty to encourage him back up, before she abruptly flattened herself to the rocks, cowering and whining.

"What's there?" she asked, thinking of bears and snakes and bobcats. "What is it, Jake?"

He raised a palm, indicating that she should keep back. "It's—oh, God, no. It's—" For all his earlier calm, his voice was shaking now, hollowed out by horror. "You don't—Liane, you don't need to see this."

More than his words, his tone launched her into motion. Climbing to his level, she came up behind where he remained on hands and knees, only now he was leaning forward, reaching toward something between the boulders.

Her every heartbeat crashed like thunder. Her lungs

seized even before she consciously registered the pair of khaki cargo pants, the bent knee and the booted foot.

Jake's back and Misty's bulk blocked the rest, but still, she knew that she was looking at the crumpled form of a man. A man half-hidden by the rocks he'd fallen down between. A man wearing the same clothing, the same style and brand of boot, as her...

But that was impossible. It couldn't be the father who'd served as her bedrock, her lodestone. The father who'd invited his broken daughter and two scared kids to come home after the trial was over, brought them home and coaxed them patiently back to life.

"Dad!" she shrieked, tears stinging as she tried to push into the narrow space beside Jake. "Out of the way, Misty!"

She shoved the dog aside and saw red, the red of blood covering the torn neck and soaking through his shirt. Her dad's plaid shirt, one of his favorites.

"No," Jake warned, taking her by the shoulders and turning her away. "I told you to stay back. He wouldn't want you seeing him like this."

"But we have to help him," she cried. "Move! You have to let me see."

With Misty pacing and crying piteously behind them, Jake shook his head. "I'm sorry, Liane. I'm so sorry. But your dad—your father's gone."

At his confirmation of her fears, Liane began to sob. Half for what she'd seen already and half for what she hadn't. Because as frantically as she looked around, she found no sign of her children. No indication of whether whatever wild beast had done this to her father had dragged them off, as well. Or had the two of them, both unfamiliar with the area, run blindly on their panicked mounts? Or were her babies trapped or lost in some remote corner of the canyon?

The nightmare image replayed itself, her vision of her children surrounded by flames and crying for her. Her son and daughter dying, frightened and alone.

She screamed her children's names, and when no answer came, her calls morphed into keening, like a wounded animal's cries. Grief and terror mingling and reverberating from the rock.

"Liane, please." Rising, Jake reached for her and pulled her into his strong arms. Pulled her close against him. "Please, don't…"

Unable to bear being touched, she struggled free. "Don't tell me what to do. What to feel. He's—he's my father. They're my children."

"That's right. And now your kids are going to need you to find them. Your dad—your dad would want you to—" His voice broke, but he quickly pulled himself together. "You know damned well he'd tell you to pull up your bootstraps and get yourself in check. He'd kick your rear if he had to—just the way he did mine after last year's fire—and remind you to attend to what needs to be done."

She stared at him, allowing his words to filter past her shock. Her father was gone. With his body lying so close, there was no way to deny it. But Jake was right about what her dad would say, what he'd said to her after the shooting.

Cody and Kenzie needed her, more right now than ever. And without their grandfather to rely on, they had no one else. No one except her and the help Jake Whittaker had offered. It was little enough to stand against a wild animal's hunger and an even more dangerous forest fire.

"We'll find them," she vowed. "We'll bring them home alive."

Because she would go mad if she considered any other possibility.

* * *

Despite his exhaustion, Cody jerked awake, heart pounding, at the sound of Kenzie's coughing. He had no idea how long he'd been asleep, or how late it had been when he and his sister had sunk down into a hollow thick with scratchy pine needles just to rest a minute. Huddling together for warmth, they'd dropped off almost instantly.

Now Kenzie was wheezing and needed her inhaler. But the first aid kit was packed on Grandpa's mule, and he had broken free with both the horses and run off, after...

Blinking back tears, Cody started coughing, too, the smoke nearly choking him. Smoke that had gotten so much thicker while they'd been sleeping.

And smoke meant a fire somewhere. He couldn't see one anywhere around them, but that didn't mean it wouldn't find them if they didn't move.

"C'mon, Kenzie, wake up," he urged, reminding himself that he was the big brother, so it was up to him to take care of her, to get his little sister home and back to their mom. "We've gotta go. We have to hurry."

She murmured, rolling away, and he heard her burrowing deeper into the dry needles. That was one thing about Kenzie. She could make a nest and conk out absolutely anywhere.

"Get up," he ordered, trying to sound as stern as Grandpa when they didn't wake up for school after the first two times they'd been called.

At the thought of Grandpa—of the moment he had taken his eyes off the bad man and shouted *"Run!"*—Cody's stomach pitched, and he thought he might throw up.

But he didn't, couldn't, just like he couldn't let himself cry. Because crying would make his eyes sore and his throat hurt, but it wouldn't do a thing to help them.

Still, he couldn't stop remembering, couldn't help thinking of what he'd glimpsed or how he'd grabbed Kenzie by the hand and dragged her into the thickest woods, sticking his palm over her mouth to keep her from screaming....

To keep *him* from finding them. From taking them away and maybe hurting *them,* too, because he'd sounded so mad when they hadn't answered his yells.

Scary mad, just like Cody remembered from two years ago, even if Kenzie had been too little to know what he was like.

Wiping his hot eyes with his sleeve, Cody gave his sister a shake. "Come on, Kenz. You've gotta move now, or you'll be late and we'll both be in trouble."

"Wanna sleep!" she burst out. "Leave me 'lone, Cody. It's still dark."

"It's the smoke," Cody said. "It'll make your asthma real bad if we stay here. And Grandpa said to get home, to find Mom and tell her what happened."

Kenzie jerked her skinny body upright, her short sparkle-polished nails digging in as she clung to him. She hiccupped a little, the way she always did when she cried, and her breathing came in noisy little gasps.

"Cody, we hafta go back and find Grandpa so he can take us home on Buttercup and Arrow."

"I don't know where they are," he said, wishing so hard that they still had the fat and fuzzy palomino or Arrow, his favorite. Or even Grandpa's giant mule, but there had been no time to do anything but run and run, then crawl beneath the low branches of a laurel and make themselves as small as two mice, wishing that Grandpa would come and find them. But they were alone, which meant he was in charge. Which meant he had to make Kenzie listen, whether she wanted to or not. "We're going to have to walk."

"How far?"

"Not too far," he lied.

"No. I want Mommy," she whined, then started coughing again.

"If you come with me, I'll take you to her."

"But we're lost. How will you find her?"

"I just will," he swore. "You'll see. And then she'll tell Mr. Jake to get his hotshot friends to go help Grandpa."

"Buttercup, too?"

"All the horses," he said, and it seemed to calm her down a little.

Peeling his sister off him, Cody felt around for the fat stick he'd picked up yesterday. A walking stick, like Grandpa might use. Then he took his sister by the hand and started moving forward blindly.

Listening to her wheezing grow worse with every step.

Jake sucked in a breath through clenched teeth and dragged his gaze from Liane's father. There was nothing he could do for Deke. Nothing beyond getting Liane's family—the family the older man had undoubtedly defended to his last breath—back to safety.

"We have to go," Liane said. Clearly in shock, she slipped off the red jacket she was wearing, her movements stiff and jerky as she thrust it toward him.

"Cover him with this, please," she said. "Cover up his face."

Jake shook his head. "You'll need it. It's still chilly. And there could be burning cinders, too."

"I can't—we can't just leave him out here like this. What if it comes back, whatever did this to him? What if it decides to—"

He laid a hand on her arm. "A jacket wouldn't stop an animal, but the lack of one could stop you."

As she peered down toward the body, Jake shifted to block her view. He didn't want her seeing Deke's face, didn't want her to remember the way death had caught him, midscream, terror written in his blue eyes.

It must have been a bear, possibly startled during feeding or separated from its young, that tore into his throat. But try as he might, Jake couldn't remember any other cases of the area's black bears actually killing anyone, and there hadn't been a grizzly seen around here in decades. Maybe a mountain lion, then, one that had set its sights on Deke's mount, but those attacks were incredibly rare, too, and other than the fatal neck wound, he'd seen no other bite or claw marks.

Chills shot up his neck as he considered the idea that whatever had killed Deke was no animal but instead some depraved individual who had used the isolation of the mountains as cover for dark deeds. Because aside from some random lunatic, who would want to kill Deke Mason? Or could Cody and Kenzie have been the real targets, with their grandfather nothing but an obstacle to be disposed of?

The longer Jake thought about the possibility of a child predator, the sicker he felt. Now that he'd allowed himself to consider the chance that the attacker had been human, he was pretty sure that either a blade or a bullet could have caused the wound to Deke's throat. And he and Liane had come out here without a gun.

"Let's go," he said grimly. "We're almost to the top, but first, put on your jacket."

He waited, prepared to offer his own jacket to cover Deke's face if she balked. Instead, after one last glance in the direction of her father, she said, "C'mon, Misty," slipped on the jacket and started walking, her shoulders shaking with her quiet sobs.

As she turned away, a practical thought cut through Jake's shock, prompting him to squat down to check his old friend's pockets in the hope that he might have been carrying Kenzie's inhaler. Finding nothing—not even a wallet—he caught up to Liane and reached for her again, as much because he needed to receive comfort as to offer it.

She didn't pull away when he put his arm around her.

Liane paused, looking behind them. "Misty, *come*."

Whining in agitation, the dog swung her attention back and forth between Liane and the man she'd worked with, lived with and followed nearly everywhere since she'd been a pup. With her tail tucked between her legs and her head lowered, she finally made the decision to obey.

The hike was steeper and longer than Jake had thought, so by the time they reached the ridge a leaden smudge had lightened the eastern horizon. But the brightest illumination they saw lay to the west, where a hellish orange flickered, reflecting off the low gray bellies of thick banks of smoke.

Elk Creek Canyon was ablaze in half a dozen places, with thousands of towering trees going up like matchsticks. Jake knew that before help could arrive the fires would unite, then run rampant, destroying the forest and the thick carpeting of branches and leaf litter, and blackening every rock.

A part of the life cycle of this land, such purges were considered vital to the forest's health, especially after a long drought. But priorities changed when they put human life—particularly the lives of a pair of children—at risk.

Letting go of him, Liane cupped her hands around her mouth and shouted, "Kenzie! Cody! Can you hear me?"

When she paused, her own voice echoed back. But there was another sound, as well, a breeze rattling through dry foliage and blowing toward them. Hot and thick with ash, it might have been a breath straight out of Hell.

"Cody! Kenzie!" Jake yelled, his deep voice rolling like thunder. Neither of the children answered.

"Try your phone," he told Liane, hoping that with the higher elevation they might be able to get a signal and make contact with the authorities. "I'll try mine, too, and the radio."

Pulling the phone out of his pocket, he winced when he saw that the battery had died. The radio was still working, if anyone was close enough to pick up his signal.

He tried channel after channel, broadcasting their names and approximate location, along with a request that any listener call for emergency assistance. For a few minutes he thought someone might be attempting to respond, but then he realized he was hearing one side of a conversation regarding another search and rescue operation on the north slope of Bear Mountain.

"Jake," Liane said, "I couldn't get a call through, but I sent a text to my boss."

"You reached Em?" Jake had known the lodge owner for years, had even dated the tall blonde a couple of times before he'd figured out that she was a firefighter groupie, a bored rich woman intent on sleeping her way through the ranks. Though for years his relationships with women had been no better, he had finally come to a point when the futility of that approach had put him off.

But as shallow as Emma was when it came to relationships, he was confident she would act on Liane's message if she received it.

Liane nodded. "She texted back, said she's calling the sheriff right now so he can send help. I gave her our location and told her the kids are out here somewhere."

"That's great," he said, and he meant it. But as he looked back toward the fires, he was disturbed to see how much closer the nearest blaze was. Since fire always traveled faster uphill, it would only pick up speed as it moved toward them. "But the bad news is, we can't wait around for help to get here or we'll be overtaken. We're safest heading back down the way we came."

She turned a panicked look back to the forested canyon below them. "What if my kids are down in there, Jake? How can I—they'll be burned alive."

He knew she was right. If they were still alive, those two small children—the adorable kids he'd grown so attached to—would almost certainly burn, or succumb to smoke and heat. But he had no way of knowing whether they were there at all, much less *where,* much less any way of knowing if they were even still alive.

All he could say for certain was that he and Liane were both still breathing. And that they wouldn't be for very long if they failed to retreat.

Sheriff Harry Wallace had spent half his night on the phone, calling in every off-duty deputy, badgering search and rescue to get a copter in the air as soon as possible, and coordinating possible evacuations with the new captain of the local hotshot fire crew.

To no one's surprise, blazes had sprung up all over the damn place, but crews were being sent to fight only those that threatened human habitations. To make matters worse, the Masons and Jake Whittaker weren't the only people who'd gone missing. The list included a pair of backpackers who'd chosen the worst time possible to take their first hiking trip into the backcountry.

He was still on the phone, arguing that the Masons needed to be top priority, when Camille burst into his office. Two red splotches, bright as hand slaps, stained her freckled cheeks.

Though he knew she had to be exhausted, her green eyes sparkled with excitement. Dancing from one foot to the other, she couldn't even contain herself until he finished with his phone call and burst out, "It can't be him! McCleary's not here! So none of this was my fault after all."

"What the devil? No, not you, Jerry, but I'd better go see what this girl's carrying on about." Hanging up the phone, he stared at Camille and barked, "Explain yourself."

"Fred Richards emailed you."

"He didn't call?" Harry had been trying half the night to reach the man from the Nevada Department of Corrections who was coordinating the search for Stephen "Mac" McCleary, and Richards had responded with an *email?* Harry loathed computers, which never seemed to do anything he wanted. He especially hated being blown off with some newfangled memo when what he really wanted was an old-fashioned conversation—and an explanation for how an attempted murderer had managed to escape custody with three other felons and elude pursuit for days.

"I printed it out for you," Camille said defensively.

After fishing his glasses from his shirt pocket, he snatched the paper from her hand and skimmed the message, which stated that McCleary and his coconspirators had stolen a cell phone and credit cards from an elderly homeowner they'd burst in on only hours after their escape. Unfortunately for the escapees, their victim had managed to crawl to another phone before succumbing to injuries from a brutal pistol-whipping. Since that time, Richards wrote, a multi-agency task force had been hot on the heels of the convicts, who had been using both the credit cards and the cell phone—until those items were finally found discarded to the southeast, just over the Arizona border.

Since one of the fugitives, Juan Carlos Guzman, had family in Mexico, Richards and his task force were act-ing on the theory that the group was making a beeline for the border.

"So where's the proof," Harry muttered to himself, "that the four of them are still together?" In his experience, alliances among criminals were about as stable as the weather, and just as dangerous for everyone involved.

"Didn't you see that last part?" Camille chirped, clearly convinced she was off the hook for her incompetence. "The part where he says he's absolutely confident they'll have all four in custody in no time?"

"Spoken like a true bureaucrat," Harry grumbled, not believing a word of it. The more he thought about it, the more certain he was that McCleary had to be here. Nothing else made sense, especially considering what Harry knew about Mac's motives. "Email him back, why don't you, Camille? See if Mr. Computer Expert can be convinced to pick up the damned phone."

"But what do you need to talk to him for?" she asked.

"I want him to pull whatever strings he needs to get some manpower out here and help me find the Masons—" furious at being questioned, he pounded his fist down on top of his desk hard enough to topple a messy stack of unfiled paperwork "—while there are still any living Masons left to find."

Chapter 5

With all the billowing smoke, Mac had no way of knowing where Smash and Goose were, but they had to be mad as hell that he had managed to steal the rifle from their sporting-goods haul and then leave them in the dark of night. He only knew he'd lost them for the moment, and that they would kill him for certain if they ever managed to catch him.

As far as he was concerned, if the cons who'd come with him became hopelessly lost and burned to death in this unfamiliar territory, so much the better. From the moment he'd felt the shallow bite of Guzman's knife at his throat, every lie he'd ever told himself had fallen from his eyes like scales.

What was left was cold reality. The high cost of his stolen fortune. The pointlessness of his struggle to reclaim it. The legacy he would leave behind: a son who had grabbed his sister, then screamed and run from him as if he were a monster.

Without his help, they would undoubtedly die out here. Worse, would die hating and fearing him, never understanding that their grandfather had forced his hand by reaching for a weapon—not to mention that the old bastard had stolen the money Mac had skimmed off the top of his own boss's far more extensive fraud in order to secure his family's future. But maybe if he found and saved his children now, he might still have time to explain things.

There might even come a day when they would be proud to claim him as their father.

The idea took hold in his imagination, giving him the strength he needed to push forward, along with the determination to destroy anything or anyone who got in his way.

Glowing cinders rode the wind at least a half mile ahead of the flames, tiny fireflies that ignited grass and foliage wherever they alighted. Liane stared at their approach, horror hollowing out her heart.

A huge pine caught fire not fifty yards away, its branches going up with a loud *whoosh,* followed by the crackling of flames feasting on dry bark.

Time was almost up. She cried her children's names again, desperation breaking her voice. And as a crimson dawn touched the horizon, she saw the gleam of moisture in Jake's eyes.

"We have to go now," he said. "I'm sorry, Liane."

"Wait!" she cried, freezing at another sound, carried by the wind.

A voice. A child shrieking, "Mommy!"

There. She heard it again. It was Cody. She would swear to it.

"Cody! Kenzie!" she shouted, racing downhill in the

direction of the sound, with Misty racing just ahead. They were racing straight downhill, toward the fire.

"Wait!" Jake called after her. "Not that way. Over here."

Drawn by the sound of her son's voice, she didn't stop to look where he was pointing.

She was shocked when he caught up moments later, grabbing her arm and physically turning her to her left, toward an as yet untouched section of woods.

"This way!" he shouted above the crackling of dry tinder. "They're over there. You see that?"

She jerked her gaze toward the spot he was indicating and made out movement in the shadows. But from this distance she couldn't even be certain it was a person, much less one of her kids. "Cody?" she called.

Though there was no answer, she broke loose from Jake's grip and started to run. Jumping fallen limbs and scrambling over rocky outcrops, she picked up speed with the downhill incline.

She heard Jake not far behind her, but his progress over the rough terrain was slower as he picked his way among the debris. Though he urged her to wait for him, she pulled farther ahead....

Only to come to an abrupt stop when Misty planted her feet and started barking, the hair along her spine bristling in a stiff ridge. That was when Liane realized that the person trotting toward her wasn't Cody but a grown man, his features hazed by smoke and distance.

Before her mind could fully grasp what she was seeing, nausea seized her and she screamed in horror. It was impossible, unthinkable, that *he* could be a part of this. But the broad shoulders, the loping gait—the certainty ripped through her that this was the same figure that had rushed at her out of a thousand other nightmares, except this time he was real.

"Mac!" What was he doing out of prison?

"They ran from me. Hid out here," he called, his voice strained and gravelly. "Help me find the kids. I heard their voices—over this way."

How could he have gotten here, much less tracked her family to the canyon and—with a horrifying jolt of insight, she realized that he must have been the predator that had surprised her father. That had *killed* her father, who never would have let Mac within a mile of the children. In fact, he probably would have shot him on sight if he hadn't been taken unaware.

Now Mac meant to kill her, too. Kill her and take the children, or maybe murder them, too, unless she could get away from him and save them.

From behind her, Jake shouted her name, but her attention remained riveted on Mac. Though she still couldn't make out his face, his intent was clear as he charged toward her like a maddened bull, a rifle in his hands.

Her instincts screamed that he was about to take aim at her, that he'd come all this way to finish what he'd started in that hotel room in Las Vegas.

"No!" she shrieked, changing course abruptly, zigzagging back toward the fire in the desperate hope that the smoke might hide her.

In moments she was picking her way among burning trees, her lungs rebelling and eyes watering, her skin stinging with the heat.

Behind her, she heard yelling and then the boom of gunfire, followed by a shout. Jake! She swallowed a sob, sickened that Mac might have killed again to keep Jake from rushing to her aid.

A closer cry came from her right. "Mommy!"

Startled, Liane slid to a stop so quickly that her own

momentum nearly toppled her. "Cody? Cody, is that you, baby?"

She held her breath, praying for an answer. Praying that her child's voice was more than a dream-come-true trapped inside a nightmare.

Bullets flying past him, Jake shouted and dropped to the ground and landed facedown, then held himself motionless. His brain was racing, though, factoring the progress of the deadly wall of fire with the appearance of the man—and Liane's terrified reaction.

The stranger she'd called Mac had used her name, then talked about the children, who still bore the last name McCleary. Which meant this must be the ex-husband, the man she'd met after leaving him behind and heading off to find a new life.

But whatever else he was, the bastard had to be Deke Mason's killer. And Liane clearly considered him more dangerous than the inferno.

Jake looked around before climbing to his feet, the canister of bear spray in his right hand. Apparently Mac had resumed chasing Liane after deciding Jake was no threat.

"We'll see about that, you son of a bitch," he ground out, then took off running, praying he could catch McCleary before Liane became his next victim.

Plunging into the thick smoke, Jake was immediately forced to leap a patch of burning weeds as the fire chewed its way closer to him. With a grunt of pain, he landed but somehow managed to avoid falling on the blackened, smoking ground.

All around him, he heard crackling as falling cinders made huge torches of the scattered clumps of bushes. The heat pushed him back several times, forcing him to alter course.

From somewhere nearby came the echo of Misty's frantic barking. Was Liane trapped ahead?

Wiping soot from his watering eyes, he spotted movement, a figure silhouetted against flame. A split second later a buck bearing a huge rack of antlers came bounding past him, leaping over rocks and paying him no heed. Though both training and instinct urged Jake to follow the animal to safety, he was too committed to his course to turn back now. Continuing into the maelstrom, he made out something else, something moving on two legs this time, and he quickly saw it was Mac.

A dark-haired man armed with a rifle, he moved in the direction of Misty's barking. He never noticed as Jake braved blistering heat to cut between two burning spruces in an attempt to head him off. But unlike him, Mac had two good legs, and he was moving at a clip Jake couldn't match. As his quarry pulled away, Jake spotted Liane in the distance, leading her children by the hand.

Torn between relief that she had found them alive and fear for their safety, he continued moving toward Mac as quickly as he could manage.

"This way!" Mac stopped as he shouted at Liane. "Come this way or you'll get us all killed."

Did the man mean to murder his ex-wife or save her? Jake hesitated, confused, but Liane seemed to have no question. Picking up six-year-old Kenzie and balancing her on one hip while still holding Cody's hand, she turned back uphill toward the rocky ridge, keeping as far from her pursuer as she could.

"You stupid bitch!" Mac roared, his patience at an end. "Put them down, or so help me, I'll leave you here dead, too."

Charging toward Mac, the shepherd barked frantically, providing enough of a distraction for Jake to move in from behind. As Liane's ex took aim at the dog, Jake sprang forward, tackling Mac with a flying leap.

The gun went off as Mac slammed forward with a shout, Jake pummeling his ribs. With no room to maneuver the long barrel, Mac was forced to drop his weapon to defend himself, twisting toward Jake and hammering his left eye with a crushing blow.

Pain exploded, blackening Jake's vision and buying Mac the moment he needed to scoot away and reach for his gun, his face transforming into a mask of pure rage—the face of a maniac Jake knew would surely shoot him.

Misty darted in again, snarling and snapping, allowing Jake—who could barely see out of his swelling eye— the instant he needed to come up with the canister of bear spray and fire. As the noxious cloud struck Mac's face, he screamed in agony, curling into a fetal position and clawing at his own eyes.

Jake dove for the rifle, then rolled to his feet. Almost immediately the gun flew out of his hands as Mac managed to wrap his arms around Jake's ankle and knock him back to the ground.

"I have to get to my kids!" Mac shouted, swinging blindly.

Thanks to the bear spray, he couldn't see the flames tightening like a noose around them, but Jake knew he had to feel the searing heat and hear the crackling hiss.

Pulling away, Jake rose and reclaimed the rifle. For an instant he hesitated, understanding that if he left the helpless man here, he would burn to death. *Then let him,* he thought, a vision of Deke's staring eyes and blood-soaked body roaring through his mind. Still, he found himself saying, "I've got the gun. Now stop fighting and let me help you before we both end up trapped."

"You think you're taking me in? I'd sooner burn in hell."

Twisting in the dirt, Mac whipped around, hurling a fist-sized rock toward the sound of Jake's voice.

Ducking, Jake barely avoided being struck in the head.

With one last look at the man groping for another stone to hurl, he made his decision. He was happy to risk his hide to save Liane and her children, but he wasn't going to waste another instant worrying about Deke's murderer.

With her daughter wheezing in her ear and Cody choking on smoke, Liane's only imperative was getting them to clearer air. The rocky ridge should have formed a firebreak, but a massive tree had fallen right along the crest, its flaming bulk blocking her path. As she tried to move around it, the roiling smoke forced her eyes nearly closed. Missing her footing, she lost her hold on both children as she rolled back downhill.

Scrabbling toward the sound of Misty's barking, she cried, "Cody! Kenzie!"

"Mom!" Cody yelled, attempting to pull Kenzie to her feet.

The six-year-old moaned and turned her head away but didn't get up, so Liane hoisted her daughter into her arms the minute she reached them and told Cody, "Here. Hold on tight to my belt. We have to get out of the trees and onto the rocks."

But which way was it? Disoriented by her fall and the smoke that made the day as black as midnight, Liane was confused. So she sucked in a deep breath and took off in what felt like the right direction, praying she'd guessed right.

She wanted to cry out for help, but she was terrified of drawing Mac back to them. Terrified and confused, because he'd undoubtedly killed her father and might very well have shot Jake, too, yet he had sounded desperate to get the children to safety.

Had she been wrong to flee him, to risk losing Cody and Kenzie to the fire? Had she cost her children their best chance of survival out of fear for her own life?

As she blundered forward the burden of her daughter's weight slowed her steps, and her thoughts were slowed, too, by the lack of oxygen. Suddenly aware that she could no longer feel Cody's tug at her belt, she reached back for him.

But her firstborn child had vanished, along with the dog.

A jolt of pure electric panic ripped through her. She forgot about Mac and cried out, "Cody! Misty!" and frantically scanned the area, blundering through the smoke on muscles recharged by adrenaline. When no one answered her repeated calls she choked on a sob, on a pain so intense it felt as if some unseen hand had gripped her heart, then wrenched it from her body.

Then she spotted movement to her left, no more than a fleeting shadow in the thick smoke. Convincing herself that it must be—had to be—her son, she followed, hanging on to Kenzie for dear life.

His mom was going the wrong way. Cody had to tell her. Had to get her and Kenzie up to the rocks where they would be safe. 'Cause Grandpa wasn't here, so they were his responsibility.

When Cody tried to yell at her, all that came out was a lot of coughing. His eyes were burning, and his arms and legs felt heavy. So heavy, he let go of his mom's belt. He tugged at her jacket, but he guessed she didn't feel it, 'cause she kept right on walking.

"Mommy," he choked as he fell down, but she didn't hear him, either, and now he couldn't see her.

He tried to stand up and run after her, but he was so

tired, and it was easier to breathe down here by the ground. He remembered Mr. Jake telling him and Kenzie that if their house ever caught on fire, they should crawl out, just like babies. So he tried crawling for a while, but he was never gonna catch up like that.

Something hairy nudged him. Misty. She had come back for him. When she licked his face and pawed at him, he stood and grabbed her collar.

For a while he kept walking with her, not knowing and not caring which way she was leading him. Then, finally, he fell again as his legs gave out.

Chapter 6

It would be so much easier to lie down, to allow the smoke to blanket her and then drift off into darkness. Off to a place where she knew her father would be waiting. Maybe Cody, too, by now, since she'd lost him somewhere. And Jake, who had surely sacrificed his own life attempting to help them. Who had deserved far better than the cold shoulder she'd offered him. Who had, at the very least, deserved the whole truth about her reasons.

In her mind's eye they smiled at her, and Cody stepped into a ray of brilliant sunshine. "Come see, Mommy! There's no smoke here. Look how shiny everything is."

But Kenzie's persistent wheezing kept Liane moving beyond the trees, a climb that burned her muscles and tormented her lungs. *Just a few steps higher,* her mind repeated in an endless loop. *Just a few steps more...*

With a groan, she sank to her knees, her body quivering with exhaustion. Laying Kenzie on a nearby flat rock, she brushed the tangled tawny hair from her daughter's ash-smudged cheek. With no medications on her, there was nothing she could do, nothing except get her daughter to a hospital before she passed the point of no return.

"Sweetie, wake up," Liane urged, tears streaming down her face. "I need you to walk a little. Please, Kenzie, open your eyes. I can't…"

Kenzie coughed, her clumped lashes fluttering. "Too tired," she finally rasped, and when Liane tried to lift her, her daughter remained limp and listless. Was it simply exhaustion, or had the combination of heavy smoke and asthma deprived her brain of too much oxygen?

Looking down the slope, Liane could see that her effort hadn't been sufficient. They hadn't made it high enough, and smoke and heat would overcome them if they didn't move. So she breathed a silent prayer for strength and staggered to her feet.

But no matter how she struggled, she couldn't pick up Kenzie, and she would rather die here, too, than leave a second child behind. And she would rather lose her own life than turn her back on even the slimmest chance of help from any quarter.

"We're over here!" she cried, her own fit of coughing making it almost impossible to speak above the crackling of the fire behind her. Trying again, she added, "We're halfway up the ridge! Please—we need help!"

She sat back down on the rock, her daughter's limp form cradled in her arms. Twice more she tried shouting, then stared into the smoke-charged darkness, half hoping and half dreading Mac would appear.

When, finally, a form took shape, she could only blink, her voice choking down to nothing. When Mac saw her, would he kill her instantly, or would he drag her with him to torment at his leisure?

"Please," she sobbed, "she's dying. Whatever you want to do to me, I don't care, but she needs help before it's too…"

Before her eyes, the form emerging from the smoke changed, morphing from the ex she'd been expecting into—

"Jake!" she cried, rising to hug him close. "Thank God. I thought you were—I heard the shots, and—"

"Thanks for calling out, or I never would've found you. Where's Cody?" he asked, looking around frantically.

"Lost," Liane said, her heart shattering at the thought of her son out there somewhere, frightened and alone. "I—I couldn't carry them both, and Kenzie—I told Cody to hold on to me, but when I looked back, he was gone. I thought I saw him moving in this direction, but I…I lost him. Jake, I lost my son."

Her gaze flicked toward the leaping flames, tears choking her as she thought of her child out there somewhere, terrified. Because of her weakness.

"I'll find him, I promise. But first, we need to get you out of here," Jake said, and she noticed that ash coated his skin and clothing. His left eye was swollen shut, a painful-looking mess of black and purple. After crouching to check Kenzie, he scooped her up as if she weighed nothing.

"The wheezing's gotten worse," Liane said. "I couldn't make it any farther."

He dropped his head to listen for a moment. "Did you bring an extra inhaler?"

"I—I did, but it was on the horse, too," Liane said, hating herself for her shortsightedness. Hating Mac McCleary even move.

"Hey there, Giggle Girl," Jake murmured, giving Kenzie a light shake. "Are you ready to get back home to your own bed?"

Kenzie didn't stir at all, her head tipping bonelessly against him, her lips faintly blue. Pressing his fingers to her neck, he told Liane, "Carotid pulse is weak and rapid. We have to get her out of here fast."

"But I can't leave Cody." Liane's voice broke on her son's name. "I won't."

"Your daughter needs you right now," he said. "And I need to get you both to safety so I can come back and search for him."

With that, he started up the ridge, moving so quickly that Liane could barely keep up. Moving toward a new sound above them, the propellers of a helicopter that she prayed had come in time.

Jake hurried toward the ridge, intent on flagging down the rescue chopper and getting Liane and Kenzie both to safety. Between the smoke and the terrain, there would be no landing anywhere nearby, but they would attempt a basket rescue if he could find some way of gaining their attention.

Pale and limp as Kenzie was, there wasn't a second to spare. Though the shifting wind made a gift of fresher air, he was all too aware that the damage might be done already, with the insult of heat and ash producing so much swelling in her trachea that not even pure oxygen could reach her fragile lungs.

Reaching the top of the ridge, he put Kenzie down long enough to strip off his jacket, the dark green now a mottled gray, and wave it desperately, praying that the movement would be spotted.

The helicopter continued southward along the ridge.

Panting with exertion, Liane asked, "Where are they going?"

"Didn't see us. But they'll be back. We'll need to—"

Liane peeled off her red jacket, and as the helicopter came in for another pass, she whipped it back and forth over her head.

This time the pilot saw them, and the chopper hovered so low that they were sandblasted by the flying dust and debris. But in under a minute two search and rescue personnel were lowered to assess the situation.

Recognizing a friend of his, a tall guy with red hair named Mike Stinson, Jake leaned toward him and shouted, "We've got a six-year-old female, asthmatic, with tachycardia and cyanosis. You'll need a basket for her and a harness for the mother."

"We're lifting all of you out," Stinson yelled back, while his partner radioed to have the necessary equipment sent down.

"Negative," Jake told him. "There's another child, an eight-year-old boy, somewhere nearby. I have to find him. Then I'll meet up with the hotshot crews, or—"

"Conditions are deteriorating," Stinson argued. "And you look injured. You'll have to let the hotshots or search and rescue—"

"Retired or not, I *am* a hotshot, and I'll be damned if I'll leave that boy here to die."

Hours later, propped up on pillows in her hospital bed, Kenzie wore a mask, which was delivering another noisy nebulizer treatment to loosen her lungs. She'd responded well to the first two doses, reviving as her pulse oxygen saturation rose to near-normal levels. Still, the doctors were carefully monitoring her progress, and Liane refused to leave her side.

"Here, take this." Liane's best friend and boss, Em Carmichael, pushed a cup of coffee into her free hand. The other, grimy with soot, rested on the tiny, sheet-draped lump made by her daughter's foot.

"Now drink," Em ordered gently, folding her nearly six-foot frame into another chair. Compassion filled her blue eyes, so bright in contrast to her short, Nordic-blond hair. "Your hands are freezing, and a little caffeine will do you good."

Keeping her voice low so Kenzie wouldn't wake from her doze, Liane said, "Thanks, Em. While you were getting the coffee, did you hear anything? Anything at all about Cody and Jake?"

Em swallowed a sip from her own cup and shook her head. "Remember what the nurse promised? She'll come straight here the moment anyone has news."

Liane's lips trembled, and hot moisture made her vision shimmer. "Cody was right there, Em. Right beside me. And I left him behind."

Em's fair complexion reddened as she struggled with her own emotions. "You can't blame yourself for this. I won't let you."

"I left him alone. In that burning canyon."

"Not alone," Em insisted, laying a manicured hand on Liane's shoulder. "Jake's out there, doing everything he can."

There was a certain proprietary note in her voice that had Liane tensing, hating the reminder that Jake had ever been with Em, who, for all her finer qualities, was known around town as a serial man-eater. It was ridiculous, Liane knew, to keep thinking of him as hers, as if he were no more than a cast-off plaything she might choose to pick up again at will.

As if he would ever want any part of the woman who'd once disdained him, the woman who had come back broken, both inside and out.

"But I swear to you," Em continued, "the next time I

see that man, I'm gonna plant one right on that gorgeous mouth of his. Because Kenzie needs you right here."

"I know she does, but Cody needs me, too. He's—he's only eight, Em, and he must be scared to death, lost out there with everything burning all around him."

"You had an impossible choice to make, so Jake made a command decision for you."

"What if he gets himself killed? What if they both—"

"You said yourself, Jake moved faster than you could on that new leg of his," Em argued.

"On level ground, yes, but he still gets tripped up sometimes on rough terrain, and his eye was swollen shut, like he'd been in a fight." She trembled at the thought, an image of her ex-husband, with his big fists, roaring up at her. Focused as she'd been on her children's survival, she hadn't yet spoken to anyone about seeing Mac, hadn't found the words to tell anyone what he'd done to her father.

Here in this sterile space, with its calming pale green walls and gleaming, institutional floors, the things she'd seen seemed like memories from a nightmare. Because if her father wasn't gone, Cody couldn't be lost in an inferno. Jake couldn't be rushing straight back into danger. If she didn't speak of any of it, it couldn't possibly be true.

"Jake'll be fine," Em assured her. "And he'll bring Cody back. You'll see."

"How can you possibly say that?" Liane demanded. "You didn't see how bad it was out there."

"I can say it because I believe it. And I believe it because I know what it cost Jake when he couldn't get to his men. He won't let it happen again. He'll get through the fire and bring Cody back safely—or he won't come back at all."

Jake knew the hotshots were on their way, with their Pulaski fire axes and their protective gear and helmets, but he knew, too, there wasn't much time left to save Cody. As he worked his way back down the ridge, he tried to estimate Liane's route as best he could from the direction she had pointed out, altering the track where necessary to get around fallen trees or heavier fire.

Though a few patches of clearer sky at the horizon showed that morning had broken, visibility remained poor, forcing him to stop all too often, bending over to rest his hands on the knotted muscles of his thighs and drag in ragged gulps of smoke-charged air. Wishing in vain the helicopter crew had had an air pack to spare, he shouted Cody's name, but he didn't really expect an answer. Since the boy hadn't even called out to Liane when he'd lost hold of her, the chances were high that the smoke had overcome him.

Though Cody could be unconscious, he knew the chances were at least as good that this mission was no longer a rescue but a body recovery. The thought that he might be looking for a small, charred form slashed through him like a reaper's scythe. In all the years that he'd fought fire, he had found the dead before, usually animals, small and large, who were unable to escape the fire's path. But in one case, forever seared into his memory, he had nearly tripped over the partially incinerated remains of a missing college student, a pretty twenty-year-old who'd gone on a day hike with her dog. Burnt and blackened as she had been, she barely appeared human, but he would never forget the photos his crew had been shown before they'd gone out—pictures of a healthy, vibrant brunette with her family's Labrador retriever. Or the contrast of those images with the body he'd found curled beside an old stump, as if, even to the last, she'd been fighting to hide from the flames that had consumed her. Her dog had died huddled at her side, loyal to the bitter end.

Dog. Loyal. Of course. Why hadn't he been thinking about Misty?

Instead of calling Cody, Jake began shouting the shepherd's name, hoping the animal was still alive and able to respond. Staggering beneath the burning canopy, he pushed himself to continue, though his own breathing had grown painful and fits of coughing racked his body. But he saw nothing except the glowing fire and the black wall of thick smoke. The only sounds he heard were the crackling of the hungry flames and the hiss of boiling sap, and then, suddenly…was that barking?

Jake hesitated, unsure of where the sound was coming from. "Misty?" he yelled, then tried to whistle before electric white dots blazed a sizzling path across his vision and another fit of coughing drove him to his knees.

Though dizziness pressed down on him, he knew he needed to get back up. Needed to get the hell out before he, too, became a victim. The flare of phantom pain reminded him that a ruined leg could be replaced. But there was no prosthetic that would ever mend his Liane's broken heart if he left her son out here to die.

Sheriff Wallace tapped at the door, then entered, his badge gleaming on his chest and his hat in hand. With his gray hair mussed and coffee spatters marring his khaki uniform shirt, he looked as exhausted as Liane herself felt.

"How's the little one?" he asked.

Liane ignored the question and rose from her chair to confront him. "You wouldn't help me last night. You told me I should go to bed and my family would be fine."

"Liane," Em interjected, reaching for her, then pausing to eye the sheriff critically. "Is that true? You blew her off when she called you?"

Looking a decade older than usual, the sheriff shook

his head and sighed, his gray eyes suspiciously damp behind his glasses. "Yeah, I guess it's fair to say I did. I've always figured Deke could handle just about anything the backcountry threw at him. I couldn't believe there was real trouble."

Liane turned away and rubbed her aching temples. So far she'd refused to allow the doctors to give her more than a quick once-over or do anything that would take her away from her daughter for even a minute.

"I was wrong, Liane," Sheriff Wallace admitted. "And you have no idea how torn up I am about it. You know Deke is—he was the best friend I have. But there was something I didn't know then. Something I have to tell you."

"About Mac, you mean?"

"So you know?" he asked.

"I saw him with my own eyes."

He nodded, his gaze sliding toward Kenzie. "Is she going to be all right?"

Liane managed a tight nod. "The doctors think so. But they'll keep her overnight, at least, to monitor any swelling in her airways."

"The doctors here're real good," he hastened to assure her. "But right now, we need to talk. Just the two of us, in private, where we won't disturb her."

She stiffened, alarm blasting through her system. "You haven't come to tell me Cody—that he's—"

"I swear I don't have any news other than we've got people in the air and on the ground—and best of all, you've got Jake Whittaker out there looking for him. If anybody can get your son home safely, I'd put my money on it being him."

"You aren't just saying that to make me feel better?"

"I figure nothing can make you feel better right now,

short of having both your kids safe in your arms. But there are things we need to talk about, things that can't wait. So could you come with me for a few minutes, just down the hall here?"

"I can't." She squeezed her daughter's hand.

"Go ahead, Li," Em said. "I'll stay with her as long as you need. And I promise, I'll come find you if anything changes."

Head aching, Liane gave in and followed Sheriff Wallace down the corridor and around a corner, to a door marked Family Room. Staring at the sign, she froze, remembering another room just like this, where she and her father had been taken years before when her mother had died of her injuries following a one-car accident. Liane hadn't been much older than Cody when it had happened.

"What's the matter?" the sheriff asked her.

"This is where they take people to give them the worst kind of news."

He opened the door and gestured toward a space not much different from a living room, with an overstuffed sofa, a few chairs and a patterned rug. There was even a small TV. "Not right now it isn't," he said, his voice grandfatherly. "Right now it's just a quiet place for us to talk. I promise. Now, why don't you have a seat? Make yourself comfortable."

As she sank down on the sofa, she felt an icy flutter in her stomach. She managed a few sips of coffee, but the warm liquid couldn't touch the coldness spreading through her.

The sheriff took a wingback chair and leaned forward to say, "I need you to tell me everything, starting with what happened with your daddy."

Her breath hitched. "The rescuers found him?"

His mouth pressed in a somber line, Harry Wallace

nodded. For nearly forty years the two men had met for breakfast every Wednesday. It had been a ritual both of them held sacred.

"His body was recovered." His voice softened. "Now tell me, Liane, what do you know about how he died?"

She shook her head, hot moisture burning her eyes. "Jake—Jake found him, but he did his best to keep me from seeing. All I can say for sure is…there was so much blood, and I couldn't find my children. I called and I called them, but—"

"Let's start from the beginning, shall we? Tell me everything that happened after our conversation last night."

For the next twenty minutes Liane spoke woodenly, as if she were recounting a movie she'd seen last week, a story that had nothing to do with the children who were her life, the father who had been her refuge, and Jake Whittaker, her first love and a man who owed her nothing, yet had risked everything to help her. She knew from past experience that the numbness wouldn't last, that eventually she would be forced to deal with the rage, the grief, the devastation—that all of it would send her crashing to the bottom of the well she'd spent years crawling out of.

Except that this time she couldn't imagine finding the strength to climb out on her own.

Panting with exertion and slick with ash-streaked sweat, Jake fought his way toward Misty's barking. As he pushed through thick brush, some thorny horror snagged his artificial leg and sent him sprawling, the prosthesis twisting painfully below his natural knee.

As he struggled to reposition the leg and get up, it sank in that he'd been deluding himself, imagining he could rehab and retrain to the point where he could once more lead his team into the backcountry. It was a goal he'd shared with no one, one so daunting that he barely allowed himself to consciously consider the possibility. Up until today, he'd thought he was making progress, getting to the point where he could do the work he had been born for instead of being sentenced to spend the rest of his life consulting Russian dictionaries for his dry-as-dust translations.

But his disappointment at this reality check was nothing compared to the knowledge that his limitations could cost Liane her son's life.

"Like hell," Jake grunted as he strained his muscles to push himself upright. Wincing each time he put weight on the bruised stump, he forced his way through a ravine so smoke-charged, he hacked until he saw stars.

If Cody was down here, he realized, he had to be dead already, but when he choked out Misty's name, her barking led him up the other side and out, where he finally spotted her standing atop a rock. Her head was low and her shaggy gray hair singed in several places, but she wagged her tail and licked at the air when she saw him.

"Cody?" he called, but there was no answer, and he saw no sign of the missing boy. His gut clenched with the thought that the boy might have gotten separated from the dog—or that she'd abandoned his small body, her instinct leading her to the relative safety of this rocky knob.

"Come on, girl. Come here," he called, voice breaking. But the big shepherd only whined and spun in circles, forcing him to climb.

He had nearly reached her when he spotted what appeared at first to be a pile of rags partly tucked beneath a ledge.

"Cody!" Jake shouted, his eyes stinging as he hobbled over and knelt, ignoring the pain, to shake the boy's shoulder. "Cody, I'm here now. Everything will be okay."

Though Cody didn't respond, his flesh was warm, thank God, and he was breathing.

"We're getting you out of here," Jake promised, grimacing as he picked up the eight-year-old…

And wondered how he would ever manage, with the added burden of the boy's weight, to make it to the ridge.

"They were supposed to warn me," Liane insisted. "They promised they would call me if he were ever released—and especially if he escaped. He's found ways to threaten me from prison. He's obsessed with the fact that I testified against him—as if I was going to keep my mouth shut after he kicked in a door and shot me. That's why I finally gave up my job and moved back home last fall."

The sheriff cleared his throat, his gaze troubled. "Have you changed your number recently?"

She shook her head, then stopped, eyes widening. "I did get rid of my old landline when we came here, but they had my cell, too. Do you think this is my fault? That if I'd updated their records, my father would still be—"

"There's blame enough to go around," he admitted with a deep frown. "The Victims Services people faxed my office. But there was a mix-up and the fax got lost. I'm so sorry."

"You're *sorry?*" She rose from the sofa, knocking over the cold dregs of her coffee as she glared into his face. "Mac *murdered* my father. And for all I know my son and Jake could both be…"

Though she couldn't force the word out, her mind screamed it. *Dead!*

"God help me, I know, Liane, and I'm not here to make excuses. But it didn't help that the Nevada people had it wrong, too. They have solid forensic evidence that McCleary was with the others when they killed an elderly homeowner not far from the prison, and they were tracking the use of the victim's credit cards and cell phone. I'm sure they'll want your statement—and probably Jake's and the kids', too—for confirmation, because everything pointed to the fact that all four men were heading south together, probably for the border."

She shook her head. "They're looking in the wrong place if they think Mac went anywhere near Mexico. He's here—probably still in Elk Creek Canyon. I hope—I hope that murdering lunatic burns to ashes."

Stifling a moan, she clapped her hand over her mouth, the thought of Mac's fate an all too visceral reminder that her son was still out there, too. "What if—" she asked, her voice strained with terror, "what if Mac finds Cody before Jake does?"

Harry reached for her, but she turned away from his touch. He sighed, then said, "Jake will keep him safe if anybody can."

"What if no one can?" She shook her head. "My father couldn't. *I* couldn't. What if—"

"Stop, Liane. This isn't helping."

She speared him with a desperate look. "*Nothing's* helping."

"Maybe not," he conceded, "but whatever happens, your daughter needs you right now. She needs you to stay strong."

She nodded, wishing there was someone, anyone, left to tell her how.

"There's something else you should know," said the sheriff. "Last night I stopped by the ranch. The power was out from the storm, but everything else looked just fine. Except for the old bunkhouse—the place was torn to pieces."

"Jake's place? That doesn't make sense. Mac's never

even met Jake. I can't imagine he even knows his name." Certainly she'd never brought up her old boyfriend to her husband, had barely allowed herself to think of the love she'd left behind. "Besides, how could Mac have broken into Jake's cabin? He was in the canyon at the same time we were."

"You're right. He couldn't have. Which means that more than likely he's brought along at least one of his fellow escapees. Somebody must have stayed behind to do the damage."

"But why wreck *Jake's* place?" Confusion spun through her mind, but try as she might, she couldn't pluck the strands of logic from the maelstrom. "It doesn't make sense."

"Usually, when places are tossed the way this one was, someone's looking for something. Drugs. Or money."

"Jake's no addict. I'd swear to it. And I can't imagine him having a lot of cash lying around. Besides, if that's what they were after, why not break into the big house?"

Harry Wallace shrugged. "Could be the alarm deterred 'em. Or maybe they were interrupted."

"I still don't understand it."

Harry's gaze was deeply troubled. "I can't explain it, either. But I swear to you, Liane, I'll figure this out."

Before she could respond, someone rapped at the door so insistently that they both jumped to their feet. In a moment Em stepped inside, her face flushed.

"Is it Kenzie? Is she all right?" Liane asked.

"She's fine, just resting. It's Cody—he's been found. They're airlifting him straight here."

"Oh, thank God. But—" Liane could barely force the questions out, she was so frightened of the answers. "Is he alive? Hurt? And what about Jake?"

Em shook her head. "All I heard is they're administering first aid on the copter. And first aid means you're alive, right? They wouldn't give Cody first aid if he were—"

"Let me go find out," the sheriff said as he hurried to the door. "I'll be back as soon as I've got something to report."

Knees shaking too hard to support her, Liane sank back down on the sofa and prayed that whatever news he brought her would be something she could bear.

Chapter 7

Jerking awake, Jake instinctively reached down, his mind catapulted back to the horror of regaining consciousness to find his lower left leg gone. Pain pinched at his right arm. Opening his right eye—the left was swollen shut—he saw that he was connected to an IV hanging just beside his bed. Bed? How had he gotten to the hospital so quickly, and what the hell was strapped over his face?

He thought back, struggling to put together what had happened. His memories were a jumble of fragmented images of fire and smoke and throbbing pain in his knee.

When and how had he been found? Had Micah come after him, digging him out from beneath the tree? And what about his men? Had someone gotten them out safely?

No, that part was all wrong. That had happened last year. Today he had been searching for Liane's son, for Cody, that unmoving, huddled shape he remembered shaking to no avail. Dead, Jake thought, though the details remained hazy.

And where *was* he? How had he gotten here?

He tried to curse but only coughed. Once he started, he couldn't stop, so he was grateful when someone—a nurse?—hurried in, elevated his bed and held a glass of water for him.

"Here, let me lift your oxygen mask a minute, so you can take a few sips."

As she made the adjustment and put the straw to his lips, he turned his head to see her out of his good eye, and took in the unraveling brown braid over her shoulder and the swollen blue eyes. Liane's eyes, sore from weeping, yet here she was, by his side, helping him despite her losses.

Unable to speak, he sipped the water. As his coughing subsided, a raging thirst rose up, prompting him to drink deeply.

"Not too fast or you'll be sick," she cautioned him gently as she pulled the cup away. When she tried to reposition the mask, he pushed her hand aside.

"I'm so sorry," he croaked, his voice sounding like the scraping of dried twigs over gravel. "So sorry—I tried. But I couldn't—"

He remembered struggling forward, pushing past endurance, until he'd found... And he'd done it for Liane, the woman he now realized he had never entirely stopped loving. The woman he had failed, just as he'd failed his men.

"Don't, Jake. Please don't apologize," she answered, fresh tears streaming down her face. "There's nothing to be sorry for. You could have been killed out there."

"But Cody..."

Her face was smudged and tearstained, and she stank of smoke as badly as he did, but her smile was the most beautiful thing he'd ever seen. "Don't you remember? Cody's going to be fine—because of you. The search and rescue people say you even managed to get Misty back to the ridge before you collapsed. She's at the vet clinic right now."

"They're both—I *found* them?" Even as he asked the question, the jigsaw images snapped together. He remembered, as if from a dream, how Misty's barking had finally led him to find Cody, how the boy had finally responded to his efforts to revive him.

"And Kenzie? How is…?" He paused to catch his breath. "How's her asthma?"

"She's much better now. Em's with her and Cody. They're both under observation." Her voice broke as she bent to wrap her arms around him and touch her lips to his temple. "Thank you so much. It's horrible enough, facing what happened to my father. But if my kids hadn't made it, there's no way I could have—you risked everything to save all our lives, Jake, and I swear to you, I'll never forget it."

As she pulled back, he raised his untethered hand to brush away her tears. "I only wish… I'm sorry. So sorry about your dad."

"They found…they got my father out of there, too." She pressed her trembling lips together as she fought for control. When she could speak again, she said, "I told the sheriff about seeing *him* out there."

"Your ex-husband?" he asked carefully.

She nodded, her eyes stricken. "Sheriff Wallace says that Mac escaped."

"He was in prison?" Jake asked.

"Yes. They sentenced him to twenty years in a penitentiary in Nevada for attempted murder."

"Whose?"

Shaking her head, she said, "Let's just say I picked the wrong man, as wrong as you can possibly get."

"It was you, wasn't it?" he guessed. "The bastard tried to kill you. Why am I just now hearing about this?"

"He did," she said. "Fortunately the media doesn't consider domestic violence cases nearly as interesting as celebrities with roaming hands. And I begged my dad to keep it quiet. I couldn't stand the thought of being stared at, whispered about and pitied for my mistakes," she said, "especially since it's everyone else who's suffered for my mistake. My children and my father. You." Gingerly, she touched his cheek, beneath his injured eye.

"There was a fight," Jake admitted, gritting his teeth as he remembered, "but a face-full of bear spray settled it. Liane, I don't see how he could've possibly gotten out of there alive, blinded the way he was. I gave him the chance to come out with me, but he seemed a lot more interested in taking off my head."

"If he died out there, I can't be sorry, not after what he did."

Jake nodded, his stomach spasming as he remembered the shock of finding Deke's corpse.

She put down the water and hugged herself. He ached to gather her into his arms and say something to ease her pain. But she turned from him, just out of his reach. And no wonder, when the man she had once fully trusted had repaid her faith with a bullet.

"You'd think a man who'd just broken out of prison—" he reached for the cup again to soothe the sting of his throat "—would have sense enough to stay as far away from you as possible. After all, isn't that the first place the authorities would come looking?"

"If they had, my father might still be alive." Shaking her head, she blinked back tears. "I do know the old Mac would have been smart enough to stay miles away from any place he might be recognized. But then, the old Mac never would have hit me, either, much less…"

Jake couldn't stop himself from asking, "How'd a

woman like you ever end up with that loser?" *Why him and not me?*

Her gaze drifted away, a blush deepening her color. "You have to understand, he was so different when I met him. He was always so considerate—he seemed to live to make me happy. He moved in fast, maybe too fast, but he kept telling me he'd waited all his life to meet me and he didn't want to waste a minute."

"Sounds controlling to me."

"That's what Dad kept saying, but I wouldn't hear it. I was too busy pinching myself, thinking I was dreaming that such a handsome and successful man would want to marry a girl just out of school."

Her father had told him that she had picked a rich guy. Despite what they'd just gone through, the memory of their history rose like a wall of ice between them, cold and slick and insurmountable. He might always care for her, but he would never forget how it had felt to be told she had to see what else was out there. *Who else,* she might as well have said. "And Mac was older, too, right?"

"Twelve years." She sighed, then shook her head. "I'd just taken my first job in Vegas, my dream job, or so I thought. It was so exciting, but I was alone there. I didn't know a soul."

That was your choice, he thought, but he restrained himself from speaking. *I would have given anything if you'd reached out to* me.

Even after she had told him not to wait for her, he had written to let her know that he was still here if she changed her mind. That he would be waiting for her to get her need to travel and explore out of her system.

With his grandmother's health failing, he'd been forced to stick close to home, taking distance learning and extension courses in his spare time as she practiced Russian

with him. He'd never for a moment regretted the years he
had spent caring for the sweet *babushka* who'd taken him
in after his mom's death. Her house was the only place
he'd ever felt at home.

He'd only regretted that Liane had never offered so
much as a glimmer of hope that she intended to return,
leaving him to turn to a string of short-term, strictly physical affairs to ease his disappointment. Neither they nor his
career had ever eased the hollow ache she'd left.

"If it makes you feel any better," she said, "I'll admit
it. I was stupid. I got caught up in the fantasy and let him
sweep me off my feet. He seemed so charming and sophis-
ticated—everything I thought I wanted."

He swallowed back his bitterness, reminding himself
that he'd been the one to ask her for an explanation.

She shook her head, her blue eyes misting. "At first
things seemed so right, but after we married, I began to see
how vulnerable he was behind the facade. He was always
under so much pressure to perform—these crazy quotas
from his boss, new young brokers always snapping at his
heels. And he was out at all hours, being wined and dined
by financial-products salespeople, all of them users bent
on promoting their own agenda." She closed her eyes, and
her voice grew strangely detached. "It sounds crazy now,
but I felt sorry for him. I tried and tried to help him, even
after I found out about the drugs."

"Drugs?"

"Cocaine, for certain, and heaven knows what else," she
confirmed. "In the space of a few months his personality
changed completely. He started muttering to himself, and
sometimes he stayed out all night. Other times he'd pace
for hours on end, then scream at the kids for making noise,
and me for letting them."

"Did he hurt the kids?" Anger twisted his insides at the thought.

"Never physically," she said. "I always managed to distract him."

"So he took it out on you instead?"

"Not at first. But after his old firm accused him of embezzling over two-and-a-half million dollars, he came completely unglued."

Jake couldn't help but ask, "Did he do it?"

"Even now, I don't know." She shrugged and shook her head. "He was so adamant in his denials, so freaked over what everyone was saying about him. We had FBI and Securities Exchange Commission agents on our doorstep. I should have left him then, but it felt like my family was under attack, and it *was* a sickness, what those drugs did. I couldn't kick him when he was down like that." She hung her head, her color rising. "I just wanted to believe everything would be better, *he* would get clean and get better, and I'd have my husband back again as soon as they figured out it was all a huge mistake."

Feeling the shame that radiated from her, he instinctively sought to ease it. "It's only natural to want to circle the wagons in a crisis."

"They never did find a trace of the money, and later on the whole firm ended up in serious trouble," she said. "But at that time Mac was paranoid that someone was out to destroy him. After he was fired, he drove away his friends, and then he convinced himself that I was spying on him, reporting his activities to his former boss, the government and heaven knows who else."

"You should've called your father. He would've come for you." *I would have.*

But that would be easy to say now, in hindsight. The truth was, after the way she'd left him, he would have been more likely to give her the number of a domestic violence hotline and then hang up. After all, she was the one who had insisted he move on and make his own life.

But even as he thought it, he knew he was lying to himself. If she'd picked up the phone, he would have dropped everything, done anything, to help her. To earn the chance to someday stake his claim.

"Maybe I wasn't ready to admit Dad was right about my marriage," she confessed, the words flat and lifeless. Broken. "Or that I'd stayed even after things got physical. I still kept thinking I could help him. I imagined I could save him. Stupid, huh?"

"You're not a stupid woman, Liane," Jake said, but her voice overrode his.

"Finally he really hurt me—broke my jaw and swore he'd kill me if I ever left him. He was so out of control, I was scared to death we'd all end up one of those awful stories on the news. So first chance I got, I took the kids and sneaked out."

"But Cody and Kenzie are his kids, too. How could he—"

"Before he got sick, they were. He was a good father back then, before… But later he accused me…he said I was making Cody afraid of him and Kenzie wasn't even his—just because she has my blue eyes and his boss had blue eyes, too."

"He really is nuts." Jake reached for her hand and squeezed it. "I would never believe for a moment that you're the cheating kind."

In fact, she'd been the honest kind back when both of them were eighteen. The kind who'd thought a clean break the fairer option before she went off to college.

It had been the right thing, the moral thing, to do. He understood that suddenly. So why had it taken so many

years for him to see it, and to see that he had scared her off
with all his foolish talk of starting his own—*their* own—
family right out of high school?

"Thank you, Jake," she said. "And you're right. I could
never respect myself if… I could never…"

Divorced or not, she still hasn't broken free, he thought,
since he'd never heard about her looking twice at any man
since her return home. But considering the hell she'd been
through, it was no wonder she retreated whenever a man
came near. Even the first man she had ever loved.

Now, with her father gone, he wondered if it was even
possible that she could ever learn to trust again? And was
he willing to risk his heart again to try to teach her?

"It *wasn't* my daddy who hurt Grandpa," Cody said
stubbornly. He thought his voice sounded funny behind
the oxygen mask.

His mom was sitting on the bed beside him, holding
Kenzie, who had gone all stiff and quiet when Sheriff
Wallace started asking questions. A few minutes earlier
his mom had told them what Cody knew already. That
Grandpa wasn't just hurt, he wasn't ever coming back.

Cody closed his eyes, remembering how Grandpa had
gotten down from Waco to get rid of a stone that had gotten
caught in Arrow's shoe. Then Kenzie had starting whining
about how she had to pee, and Grandpa had lifted them
both down from their horses and told him to stand guard
for her while she squatted behind a rock.

She'd barely finished when Cody heard the angry
voices, and then a gunshot. He'd peeked his head out and
shouted, "Grandpa!"

He'd been just in time to see the ketchup exploding from

Grandpa's throat. Just in time to see him fall and hear the gurgling sound he made. And then the man with the gun saw him over by the rock and shouted.

"Hey!" he'd yelled. "Hold it!" Cody knew that tone. It was the voice from his old nightmares.

"He's not my *real* daddy," Cody insisted, his fists balled tight. "He's a *bad* man. A rotten, stinking no-good piece of horse poop. I hate his guts! *I hate him!*"

Yelling made him start coughing again, and his mom leaned over and hugged him, patting his back until he finished.

"You're okay. It's okay," she said, kissing the top of his head. He squirmed away. He didn't want Sheriff Wallace to think he was a baby.

The sheriff gave his mom a look, and she nodded and sighed. "I know you want a different father, Cody," she said. "A real dad—and you deserve one. But the sheriff needs to know, was the man you saw, the man with the gun with Grandpa, was it your—"

"Was it this man?"

The sheriff took a picture from his pocket, a picture of a man Cody remembered smashing down the door, then shooting Mom and almost making her die, too. And then he'd screamed at him and Kenzie to stop their damned sniveling.

His heart filled up with hot hate, red and angry as the ketchup that he knew had really been blood. Even though he hadn't gotten a good look at the man's face, he knew the meanness in that voice, all right.

So he sat up straight and pulled the mask off so the sheriff and his mom would hear him. "It was *him,* I know it. He was the man who killed my Grandpa, the man who wanted to kill us, too. And I hope he burns up out there. I hope he burns in—" He slanted a look toward Kenzie and knew he shouldn't say the bad word in front of a first grader. So he spelled it for them instead, and his sister's eyes went wide.

Several hours later Jake picked up the photo he'd selected from the array the sheriff had spread out before him. "You bastard," he said flatly, glaring down at the squared jaw and narrow nose, the heavy brows and the resentful, dark eyes of the bastard who had nearly killed her. Relieved as he was that the doctor had pronounced him well enough to discontinue the supplemental oxygen, the situation still felt surreal, like something from a nightmare.

"You know, Jake," Harry told him, carefully changing the subject, "Deke thought the world of you. He always wished things had worked out between you and Liane. He would've been damned proud to claim you as his son."

The sheriff's gaze slid away, and Jake had to take another drink of water from the cup beside him.

"He would've been proud of the way you came through for her, too," Harry went on. "Proud and grateful, especially considering—"

"He was the best man I knew, and he would've told you—" Jake forced the words out through his tight throat "—to quit blaming yourself for not finding out about McCleary's escape until after—"

"I have plenty of reasons to blame myself, so there's no need to try to make me feel any better. I don't *want* to feel better right now. I damned well don't deserve to." Before Jake could think of what to say, Harry cleared his throat and went on. "I've recovered Deke's gun from his mule, but what happened to that gun McCleary had? The rifle he shot at you with?"

"I took it with me when I left him there, but I lost it later. Put it down when I went to pick up Cody, I guess, or…" Jake shook his head. "I don't remember. Stupid thing for me to do. I'm sure you could've used it for the investigation."

"You had a few things on your mind, I imagine."

"One or two, I guess." Jake shrugged. "But right now, all I care about is making sure the guy's no longer a threat to Liane and her family." He tapped his finger on the photo of McCleary's face for emphasis.

"That makes two of us," said Harry. "Deke never liked the son of a bitch. Said he was all surface and no substance. Only made it worse when he took her off on some fancy cruise and married her without so much as a phone call."

Jake smiled, missing Deke and his old-fashioned ways. "I suppose he wanted Mac to ask him for her hand, not just take it."

"Damn straight he did," the older man said. "And I'm sure he let Liane and Mac both know it every time they came to visit."

"Maybe that's why Deke hardly saw them. And why she didn't come home straight off, even after he tried to kill her."

"Once he figured out what was going on, Deke tried to convince her to let him come and get her. But she wanted to pull her own weight, not come crawling back. That's why no one's supposed to know about the shooting."

Jake found his fists clenching. "He *shot* her?"

"I thought— I figured Deke had told you."

"Liane just mentioned that he'd tried to kill her, but she didn't say what happened."

"After she filed for divorce, he tracked her down to a motel room where she was hiding out with the kids. Shot her and left her for dead, with both the kids scared out of their wits. Now, I ask you, what kind of an animal does a thing like that to his own family?"

"Worse than an animal," Jake said, thinking of the beautiful wife and gorgeous children Mac McCleary had betrayed. A family, thrown away. "I hope the bastard suffered when he died."

Harry nodded. "Soon as we recover a body, we'll get working on an ID pronto, even if I have to light another fire under the medical examiner's hind end."

"I just hope there *is* a body," Jake said grimly. "Because the last thing Liane and those kids need to worry about is her father's killer showing up."

Chapter 8

The ungrateful bitch had imagined he meant to kill those two babies, even the son that anyone with eyes could see was his.

The memory haunted Mac McCleary even more than the ghosts of those he'd actually killed. The half-deaf homeowner he and the other cons had surprised only hours after their escape had been ancient anyway, with a slew of prescription bottles all over his kitchen. Smash had probably done the sickly old man a favor bashing in his head before they'd given his car, credit cards and cell phone to the girls. And Deke had brought his own death on himself, first by stealing Mac's money and then by reaching for his gun.

In stark contrast, the two lost backpackers who had stumbled upon him were strong and young—and willing to risk their own lives to keep him from blundering blindly into the flames.

"Let's go, man!" shouted one hiker. Mac could barely make out his bandana-covered head. Panic pitched his voice higher, making him sound more like a boy than a grown man. "We've gotta head over this way or the fire's gonna catch us!"

"No way," his taller, darker-skinned friend argued. "I've been telling you, the car's parked north of here. That's where the road is."

The old logging road, Mac figured, remembering the second route into the canyon from a map of the area he'd studied. With their help, he could find it, then grab whatever chance came up to permanently prevent them from giving away his presence.

It was a hell of a way to repay their kindness, but he'd come too far, risked too much, to reclaim his money—and the children he now saw as his true mission—to back down.

"The trees—look up," the tall hiker shouted, and above them, Mac made out the crown of one pine after another flaring into yellow-orange brilliance.

"We're cut off!" Bandana-head cried.

Cursing the bear spray, Mac wiped his stinging eyes—just in time to see a flaming brand fall and ignite the guy's clothing.

As the fire leaped and caught the long fringe of hair beneath the bandana, he shrieked—an animal sound that made the hairs behind Mac's neck rise—and started running.

"Ryan, no! Get down! Roll!" his friend screamed, but in his pain and panic, the blazing man only tried harder to outrun his fate.

Dropping his pack, the other hiker started after him. Mac clutched at his arm shouting, "It's too late for him. But you and I can make it. Come on!"

Shoving Mac away, the second hiker took off running after his companion. Even as blurred as Mac's sight was, he soon made out the bright flare of a second human torch.

Stomach heaving, he turned away, staggered by his shock and horror, even though their deaths had solved one problem. Snagging the abandoned backpack, he struggled to find a path to safety and prayed that his only real legacy, his son, hadn't met the same fate as the men he had watched die.

Late in the day Liane received word that charred human remains had been recovered less than a mile-and-a-half from the spot where her ex-husband had last been seen. Though the body hadn't yet been officially ID'd, Harry Wallace seemed confident that Mac had paid the ultimate price for his crimes.

"Considering that he was blind," the sheriff told her, "it stands to reason that you won't ever have to worry about him again."

She wasn't so sure. "What about his friends? The three men who escaped with him?"

"I wouldn't worry too much, since you and Jake and Cody didn't see any of them in the woods and the Nevada people have plenty of evidence that at least some of them took a straight shot to the border."

"Not all of them," she said. "After all, someone tore up Jake's cabin while we were gone. What I'd like to know is why. What were they looking for?"

Harry looked away before saying, "Valuables, most likely. Jake said something about some cash and his grandfather's gold watch disappearing, and some old pain meds, too, leftovers from his accident. Whoever the guy was, once he had what he wanted, he had no reason to hang around waiting to be caught."

"I hope to heaven you're right."

He laid an age-spotted hand on her shoulder, his gaze softening. "You look exhausted, Liane. Why don't I take you on home? I'll check the place out real good to be sure everything's safe, and you can rest for a few hours while your kids are looked after here."

She shook her head. With an anxious glance toward the hospital room she'd just left, she explained, "Thanks but I'm not leaving them. They need me now more than ever, and I need to be here with them."

Besides, the thought of facing the homestead without the father who had always been there unnerved her. How would she ever manage without him? She tried—and failed—to imagine herself functioning in the wake of this new trauma, taking care of the ranch, the horses and the family business on her own.

She knew instinctively that if she didn't have her children to be strong for, the ice crystals spreading from her center would shatter, just as she would.

Seeming to understand, Harry gave her a hug and said, "You need me for anything, you call me, day or night. Even if I'm home, I promise you, I'll answer."

Too emotional to speak, she nodded.

"Soon as I find out when your father's remains will be released," he continued, "I'll be happy to help out with making the arrangements."

She tightened her arms around his soft middle before releasing him. "Thank you so much, Harry. I know I was mad before, but you were a good friend to Dad. Always."

He cleared his throat and changed the subject. "Jake Whittaker was a good friend of your Dad's, too. So I want you to promise me, for your father's sake, you won't keep the past from allowing him to help you, too."

In no condition to argue, she nodded, though she suspected that, just as her father had all too often hinted, Harry hoped that she and Jake would somehow find their way back to one another. That he could somehow forgive her for making the most disastrous choice in the history of choices.

But she had no idea how to forgive herself or to find the strength to start again.

"She's baaa-ack," Jake said as he stepped inside the kitchen with a wriggling, eager Misty still hooked to the leash. After spending three days cooped up in a cage at the vet's office, the shepherd had a clean bill of health and the energy to prove it. "Liane? Where are you?"

Unsnapping the dog's leash before she pulled him off his feet, he followed Misty as she raced past the large picture window that overlooked the forest and charged into what had been Deke's study.

"Ack! Get off me, you big lummox!" he heard Liane say just before he stepped inside the room, where she was sitting at her dad's desk and fending off a slobbery greeting.

Laughing, Jake dodged the brushy whip of wagging tail. "Sorry about that. Guess I should've taken her out for a run before I brought her inside."

"Down, Misty," Liane said, rewarding the shaggy mutt with a scratch behind the ears when she finally settled. "Yes, I'm glad to see you, too, sweetheart." She looked up and smiled. "Thanks for picking her up for me, Jake. The kids will be so excited to see her here when they get home from the movie."

"It's no trouble, really. So you decided to let Em take them after all?" Before he'd left for the vet's, Liane had been balking at her friend's invitation.

She shrugged. "Kenzie's finally stopped coughing, and the movie will be good for them. Let them forget for a few hours, maybe even laugh a little. They have a rough day ahead of them tomorrow."

Her gaze drifted to the dozens of framed photos that lined the walls. In most, family members posed on horseback, from Liane herself at various ages to both the children, even her dad, looking unbelievably young, with her mother, who was seated on an old-fashioned sidesaddle, on their wedding day. There were other pictures, too, faded black-and-white shots of long-dead relatives and old dogs, of favorite visitors who'd become fast friends.

It made sense, because when he wasn't outdoors working, Deke had most often been found in this room, the original homestead the rest of the house had been built around. Jake could almost see him, working at his desk, or leaning back and nodding to the radio he'd always kept tuned to a local country station.

Drawn by the misery in Liane's eyes, he ventured closer, his limp barely noticeable today. Swiveling her chair around, he tried to knead the stiffness from her shoulders. Instead of relaxing, she tensed. "Please don't, Jake. You've been a huge help. Honestly, I don't know what I would do without you, but right now I'm too stressed out."

"Sure, Liane. I didn't mean to—" As he backed off he caught sight of the files strewn across the desk. "Bills? I thought we'd agreed I'd help you get those in order after the funeral?"

"I know we did, but right after Em left with the kids, I got a call from the bank that Dad's account is overdrawn. And I can't find his last statement anywhere. I know he's always been a mess when it comes to filing, but I can't find *anything*."

"Which account?"

"The checking. And I'm not on the account, so they're

refusing to give me any more information over the phone until I bring in all the documentation and—"

"The hell with that. You need to call the sheriff right away," he said. "Your dad's wallet is still missing, right?"

She nodded. "And his debit card was inside it."

"What about his access code? He wouldn't keep it in there, would he?"

"I can't imagine he would, but what if Mac forced him to give up the number before he…" Her face went so pale that Jake knew she was imagining the horror of her father's final moments.

"Then that means either your ex or an accomplice got out of that canyon alive," Jake reasoned.

She rose and started pacing, her arms crossed. "What if—what if they come back here?"

"Let's not leap to conclusions. If they've gotten all the money from the account, it stands to reason they'll be long gone."

She nailed him with a look, half terrified, half angry. "Don't try to handle me, Jake, because you don't really know that. You can't."

"No, I don't," he admitted, already reaching for the phone on the desk. "So how about we find out? I'm calling Harry right now."

After hearing the facts, Harry promised to get back to them as soon as possible. "I do have some news for you, though," he told Jake. "Now that the fire's burned itself out, a cadaver dog's located a second body in the canyon."

"One of the escapees? Or did they ever find those back-packers?"

"Remains were pretty badly burned. Couldn't even be sure of the gender. And no ID, so we're back to waiting on the M.E."

Slanting a look toward Liane, who was rifling through

the contents of another folder, Jake asked, "What about the first body? Any word yet?"

"Medical examiner's waiting on dental records out of the Nevada Department of Corrections, but she's promised to get back to me the moment she knows something. She knows this case is a priority."

After finishing the call, he recounted the conversation for Liane's benefit. When she went quiet, he tried a change of subject, gesturing toward the file she held. "Find what you're looking for?"

She shook her head. "The woman at the bank told me I'll need to bring in a copy of the death certificate and his will to get access to his banking information. But I can't find anything but bills. Lots and lots of bills."

"That can wait for now, Liane. Come here, please." Taking her hand, he gently pulled her to her feet and enveloped her in his arms. Once again she went willingly, as if they'd never been apart. Despite the circumstances, it felt so right and so natural to Jake that he never wanted to let go of her again.

But she was shaking, so he asked her, "When's the last time you ate something?"

"I made French toast this morning."

"For the kids, I'll bet. Did you actually sit down and eat some?"

"I think maybe…. I don't remember."

"And what about lunch? How 'bout I make you some soup, or maybe a sandwich?"

"I don't care about food. I'm burying my dad tomorrow." Her sigh, warm and human, slipped past his bare neck.

"And what about sleep?" he asked, needing to distance himself from the sensations coursing through his body.

"And I'm talking about *really* sleeping, not just collapsing and dozing for a few minutes."

"Whenever I lie down, I hear noises," she admitted. "A footstep in the hall, a pinecone rattling off the roof, every little nicker from the horses."

"I promised you I wasn't going to let anything get past me," he reminded her. Since his cabin would take days to set to rights, she had offered him the spare bedroom just down the hall from her room. He had borrowed a handgun from Deke's gun case, mostly to set her mind at ease.

He had to admit that part of his own restlessness was prompted by the knowledge that she was sleeping so close to him. But each time he imagined her slim body slipping between the sheets, guilt roared to the surface. This was no time to fantasize about her, not when she needed his friendship and support to get through her father's funeral.

"I know," she told him, "and it does help, knowing you're right there."

God forgive him, but he ached to kiss her, to shed his own grief and distract her from hers. With his conscience shouting that it was wrong, that it would be unforgivable to take advantage, he drowned out his body's protests.

But before he could step back, she looked up into his eyes and ran her fingers along the light stubble on his jaw. "Jake…" she whispered.

That was all it took for him to dip his mouth to hers, to taste the lips he'd dreamed of night after lonely night. And in that instant he felt whole again, unscarred, with the world and all its possibilities laid out before him like a feast.

Liane responded eagerly, almost desperately, pressing herself so close that surely she must feel how hard he'd grown. But instead of pulling away, she let her lips part, her moan low and urgent as he deepened the kiss.

He slid his hand along her side, feeling curves he longed to taste, to claim right here, right now, and damn the consequences. But as he reached to clear the desk behind him, awareness seared him—he was no rank boy but a man now, with a man's obligations.

Taking her like this, burning off her grief and his own in the raw lust he was feeling, would only make things even more awkward between them than they were already. And she and her kids needed him now to help them through this. He owed it to them, and to his friend Deke, to stop himself—and her—from doing something she would regret.

When he felt the dampness of Liane's tears against his skin he finally drew back, using the excuse of pulling a tissue from the box sitting on her dad's desk.

"Here, I think you need this," he said, using it to blot the delicate skin beneath her eyes.

Nodding, she took it from him, her eyes welling with remorse. "I'm sorry, Jake. That was wrong. I can't— I don't know what I was thinking, kissing you like that."

"You're running on empty, and we're both a little— We're forgetting ourselves, that's all." For her sake, he managed to smile.

She ran a hand over her loosely braided hair. "I'm losing my mind, wishing that I'd never met Mac, that I'd never left here in the first place. If I hadn't gone away—"

"You had to," he said, and he meant it, though he, too, had blamed her for a long time. "It was never fair of me, expecting you to give up a full scholarship and your dreams to stay here and raise a family. I knew you weren't ready for that. Neither was I. Not then."

"I'm home now," she told him. "But you need to understand that it's too late. It's too late for me to—"

"You know what your dad would say to that, Liane?

He'd tell you that it's never really too late. And then he'd tell you to march your rear into the kitchen and let me feed you lunch."

Later that day, Liane had just put on a pot of water to boil to make pasta when Harry finally called.

"I catch you at a bad time?" he asked, when she mentioned turning down the burner. "If you want, I can call back later."

"No, please," she said, her stomach roiling. "Now's a good time. Tell me, what did you find out from the bank?"

"First off, there's been no theft that I can see. No activity at all on the accounts this past week, and no debit card use, either. Nothing but some automatic bill payments."

"So that's what caused the overdraft, then?"

"Right."

"That's good news, isn't it?" she reasoned. "It means I don't have to worry that anyone has Dad's debit card and PIN number, right?"

"I think it's safe to say they would've already used it if they could've. But I've had the account frozen anyway, at least for the time being."

"Good," she said, thinking she could cover the bills long enough to give them a little breathing space before she was forced to take a hard look at finances—and the future of a property that had been in her family for more than a century. A property she knew her father would never have wanted her to sell. "But I don't understand why Dad let his account get down so low. Do you think he just lost track?"

At Harry's hesitation, bands of dread tightened around her.

"I'm sorry, Liane," he said, "but it's not just the checking account. Your father was having—I don't know how to say this except to come right out with it. This tough economy's done a number on his finances."

"But business was improving," she argued. "Dad's been really busy these last few months."

"Those horses you have out there, they eat all year round. Then there's vet care, shoeing, taxes... Land value's gone up even though the economy hasn't, so the taxes are high."

"Did you know about this before? Did Dad say something to you about it?"

"Not much, but that's no surprise. Your father was a proud man, and he's always played things close to the vest."

"But why would he keep secrets from *me?*" The line went silent for so long that she finally asked, "Still there?"

"I'm still here," he said. "And we all keep secrets, Liane. Maybe he didn't want to worry you about—"

"Well, I'm worried now," she said, tears springing to her eyes. "What am I going to— No, I can't think about this right now. My dad's not even in the ground."

"I know it's overwhelming, and I'm sorry, Liane. If there were any way I could've protected you from this..."

"No," she choked out, abruptly, irrationally angry with her father for doing just that. "You were right to tell me, Harry. I don't want any surprises later."

"I should drive out," he said, "and we can talk face-to-face."

She tensed, hearing in his voice the promise of more bad news. Her heart started bumping at breakneck speed. "What else, Harry? What have you found out?"

"Is Jake there with you?" he asked uncertainly.

"He took the kids with him to feed the horses. Why?"

"I just need to know you aren't alone."

"I don't understand," she said. "Did my dad—"

"It's not him. It's about McCleary. Neither of the bodies recovered from the canyon matched your ex-husband's dental records."

She sank down onto a kitchen chair, her knees suddenly too weak to support her. A coldness enveloped her, like the fumes from a block of dry ice. She'd only been beginning to work through the fact that Mac had died after taking her father away from her, but now…

"Are you still there, Liane?" Worry tightened Harry's voice.

"So who were they? Do you know yet?"

"The M.E.'s still working on it. Could be some of the other escapees, or maybe even those missing hikers— though their car isn't where the friend who reported them missing said it'd be, so they more than likely made it out."

"What if Mac took it?"

"Since we couldn't reach the hikers or their friend, I've got an alert out for the car," Harry told her. "If anybody took off in it and he's still nearby, we'll get him. But chances are, the last thing a murderer would do is stick around the scene of his crime."

She tried to believe what he was saying, wanted to with all her heart. But she wanted her father to come back, too, to tell her everything would be all right and assure her that he'd had a plan all along for dealing with his financial issues.

Right now, though, one thing felt as impossible as the other.

With the children's help and the horses' nickers of encouragement, Jake fed each animal the measure of grain that supplemented their hay rations. He was refilling water troughs in the corral when he noticed Kenzie standing outside the stall of the only horse that hadn't returned, her head lowered and her thin shoulders shaking.

"Cody, could you cut the water?" he called to his number-one helper, who was quick to turn off the hose. Then he crossed the corral and walked up behind Kenzie, gently touching the top of her head. "Hey there, Giggle Girl. How's it going?"

Sniffling, she looked up at him, her blue eyes—so like Liane's—brimming. "Cody says Buttercup's never coming back again. He says she probably got all burned up out there somewhere."

He crouched down to put himself at her level. It was on the tip of his tongue to ease her worries with a story about a fat and fuzzy palomino running off to join a herd of mustangs, where she would take her place as lead mare and run shoeless on sweet, soft grass. But Kenzie had been there while he and Liane had spread ointment on patches of burned hide on several of the animals, and she remembered enough about the fire to understand how bad it had been.

So he let loose a long breath before saying, "You know, as much as your grandpa loved both you and your brother and your mother, he really loved his horses, too. Every one of them."

"And Waco, too," said Cody as he came to join them.

"Definitely Waco," Jake confirmed, thinking that Deke had probably loved the ornery black mule most of all. "And he was always crazy about riding."

"But Grandpa had to go to heaven," Kenzie said.

Crossing his arms in front of his chest, Cody burst out, "Because that bad man ki—"

Jake silenced him with a look and a jerk of his head toward Kenzie, a reminder that he was two years older. They'd had a "man-to-man" talk earlier about good and bad ways to handle his anger, and apparently it had sunk in, because Cody gave him a conspiratorial nod and went back to listening.

"The thing is, heaven's a long way," Jake told both of

them, "and your grandpa couldn't imagine getting there without one of his very best horses."

"So he picked my Buttercup?" asked Kenzie.

"I think that's what he did. So he wouldn't be lonely without you two and your mama."

"And Misty, too," said Cody, clearly warming to—or needing—Jake's version of the truth.

"That's right," Jake said. "He left Misty to take care of you two, and all of us to take care of each other. But I expect he was thinking Kenzie here wouldn't mind too much if Buttercup rode up with him."

"I bet he picked Buttercup 'cause she's so sweet and fuzzy," Kenzie told them, wiping away tears. "He can pet her when he gets lonely and feed her apples when she misses me."

"They don't have apple trees in heaven, silly," Cody started, before adding in an uncertain little boy's voice, "Do they, Mr. Jake?"

"Who's to say if they do? For all we know, they might have mountains of those red-and-white peppermints Buttercup always liked to crunch on."

"And ponds full of molasses," suggested Kenzie.

"And carrots growing upside down," Cody threw in, topping off the idea with a big grin. "If Buttercup's not careful, she'll get so fat, she'll fall back down through the clouds."

Both children burst into giggles at the notion, and soon they started chattering about the movie they'd seen that day.

Jake decided that instead of harps and angels, this might well be the music he would pick out for his brand of heaven. But it could never be complete until he found a way to coax Liane to add the rare sound of her laughter to the mix.

Chapter 9

Two nights after the funeral, the sounds of a soft rain awakened Liane, pulling her from the slipstream of a bittersweet dream where she'd been arguing with her father. Something about Jake, she thought, grasping at the fast-receding edges of the memory, about how the two of them had already wasted too much time.

Her face burned as she remembered how hard she'd tried to convince him to send Jake packing once she moved back home. How hard her dad had argued that he couldn't possibly turn out a friend still recovering from such a severe injury.

As often as her dad had denied it, she'd always suspected he was scheming for more grandkids—this time hers and Jake's. As she lay there with her children snuggled beside her, the thought was a painful reminder that her father hadn't been the only one with secrets. But this late at night, she didn't dwell on it, her mind already circling back to the kiss she'd shared with Jake, to the reawakening hunger she had thought was forever extinguished.

With the memory, pain twisted low in her abdomen, along with the knowledge that she could never give him what he craved. She pushed the thought from her mind and pulled Cody and Kenzie closer, kissing each sleep-warmed face in turn. She knew it was past time to move them back to their own beds, time to start them on the path to normal, but ever since their return from the hospital they'd been creeping into her room at night, cuddling against her. Needing her the way she needed to be close to them, to help keep the worst nightmares at bay.

Misty, too, was keeping close, her singed fur a reminder of the horrors she'd shared with them. In the dim light cast by the clock radio, Liane saw the shepherd stand, rising from her dog bed and moving toward the closed bedroom door.

At a scraping sound from somewhere outside, Misty growled, and Liane jerked upright in bed.

It's only the rain, she assured herself, comforted by the tapping of a branch and the plinking of fat drops against the window—the thunderstorms the weather forecasters predicted would finally quench the smoldering coals threatening to reignite the backcountry. But the thought of the fires set off an avalanche of memory, with worry hot on its heels.

Giving up on a return to sleep, she had just gotten up to get a drink of water when she heard another sound—a thump this time. Was that a clay pot toppling over on the back deck? Shivering in her robe, she catalogued the many occasions when a curious raccoon, marauding coyote or some other animal had disturbed her sleep.

It's no animal this time. It's him. As hard as she had worked to barricade her mind against it, the thought kicked her heartbeat into overdrive. Mac had finally come back to finish her forever. *And maybe both our kids, too. Unless I do something.*

Trembling, she told Misty, "Stay," and quietly crept out the door, closing it behind her.

Instantly she spotted movement, a shadowy figure rushing toward her.

Before she could scream, the man was on her, grabbing her around the waist with a powerful arm and clapping a hand over her mouth. She struggled, her bare foot kicking backward and encountering something unyielding and unnatural.

"Shhh, Liane. It's me. It's all right," a deep voice said in her ear. A familiar voice that had the tension draining away like ice water from a broken pitcher.

Jake's voice, a confirmation that what her heel had struck had been his false leg.

"You almost gave me a heart attack," she whispered as she pulled free from his hold.

"Something's out there," was his only answer. "Probably just an animal, but I thought I'd check on you and the kids before I headed downstairs to see."

She noticed he'd pulled on his jeans, along with an old sweatshirt. Or had he been sleeping fully clothed, taking his protective duties far more seriously than he had let on?

"I'm coming with you," she said. "But we'll need to grab a gun out of Dad's closet."

"Did you forget? I'm armed already—or didn't you feel that .38 tucked in my waistband?"

"And here I thought you were just glad to see me." Adrenaline had her feeling so giddy that she was backsliding into the stupid banter of their teenage years, a realization that had her burning with embarrassment.

To her surprise, he let out a quiet laugh. "I'm *always*

glad to see you, Liane. Don't you know that by now? But let's get you a gun, too, just in case. Then you go back in your room and wait with the kids while I check things out."

"I should go with you. Or maybe we should all go into my room and call for a deputy to—"

"No way. First of all, it would take at least thirty, forty minutes for a deputy to get out here—maybe longer, as thin as they're stretched. Besides, they'd confiscate my man card if it turned out to be a foraging skunk or something."

If she hadn't been so scared, she might have rolled her eyes at the foolishness of his machismo. Instead she asked, "But what if it isn't, Jake? What if it's—"

She couldn't force the name out, as if speaking it would make her greatest fears come true.

"Then we definitely don't want Cody or Kenzie waking up and coming downstairs while we're traipsing around armed," Jake said firmly. "It's your job, first and foremost, to keep them safe and calm."

Her initial impulse was to lash out, to argue that he had no right to tell her how to be a parent. But she swallowed back the harsh words as her common sense caught up.

He was right. She couldn't leave the children alone. Instead, she had to be ready with the phone in hand, in case she heard any sound confirming they had human company.

"I have my cell phone with me," Jake said. "Keep yours close, and let's put them both on vibrate so we won't be heard. Okay?"

"All right."

Jake waited in the hallway as she slipped into her dad's room, her eyes burning with the memory of the last time she'd set foot inside—to find his favorite plaid flannel shirt and jeans for the undertaker, since that was how he'd always insisted he wanted to be buried. Fighting past the grief, she flipped on the light to his walk-in closet and punched in the combination to the gun cabinet he had used to keep his weapons out of the kids' sight.

She chose his shotgun, figuring she would have a far better chance of hitting something with it than his old deer rifle. Breaking it open, she loaded both barrels and dropped extra shells into the pocket of her robe, glad for once that her father had insisted she learn the basics of shooting when she was a teen. Afterward she went back into the hall, where Jake was waiting near the top of the stairs.

He was holding his left hand up behind him, signaling her to silence. She strained her ears but heard nothing except the low murmur of thunder and a fresh downpour scouring the roof.

Touching his wrist, she whispered, "What is it?"

Before she could answer, a faint noise floated up the stairwell. The sound of something heavy being dragged across hardwood floors? Or could it be an animal but a larger one than she'd first thought, maybe even a pair of hungry black bears getting into mischief outside?

Turning his head toward her, Jake pointed in the direction of her room. Nodding mutely, she exchanged a look with him and silently mouthed, *Be careful. Please.*

In all the years she'd spent at the homestead, she'd seen or heard her father get up in the night to deal with dozens of wildlife and horse-related issues. But she had never before heard noises quite like these.

And she had never before felt such a strong sense of foreboding creeping up her spine.

Breath held as he moved, Jake descended the staircase, a pistol in his hand. Mentally, he primed himself to use it if he had to, to do whatever was necessary to keep the family upstairs safe.

Like the low growl of a great wolf, thunder rumbled outside. The rain intensified, sheets of it rattling off every outside surface. Ordinarily a storm's passage made him feel grateful to be sheltered indoors, but tonight he felt restless and uneasy.

Or had he only imagined that the last sound he'd heard had come from inside, that someone—some all too human predator—was using the first real rain they'd had in months as cover for a break-in after somehow disabling the alarm?

Jake's pulse revved when another noise confirmed his worst fears: a heavy, metallic clatter followed by a deep-voiced, indisputably human curse. The intruder was definitely inside; the voice had come from Deke Mason's study. As Jake crossed the family room toward the study, he spotted a rim of light framing the door, which had been left ajar.

Rage wound tight inside him at the idea that Mac—if he were really still alive—or one of his cohorts, or some other thieving lowlife, would intrude on his murdered friend's domain, further traumatizing Liane and the kids by breaking into the home that should be their refuge. But why? And why tear apart the study? What could the intruder be looking for?

As he pressed forward, Jake thought first of Deke, the man whose casket he'd helped carry to its final resting place. But it was Liane's frightened face that flashed before him as he reached for the doorknob, that and the memory of the terror he'd heard in her voice.

He sucked in a deep breath, steeling himself to shove the door open and shout *Freeze!* But before he could act, there was yet another clunk, followed by a harsh whisper that had him stopping to listen instead.

"Could you get any clumsier, *cabrón?*" came the heavily accented words. "She'd have to be deaf not to hear you."

"Just another minute," said the same man who'd been swearing earlier, judging from the harshness of his baritone voice. "It's gotta be here someplace. It's not like he woulda kept it in the bank."

"We gotta get out of here now. Before she gets the sheriff on us. I'm not goin' back in a cage again for no amount of money."

So that's what they're after, Jake thought. Did they imagine Deke had kept a cashbox for his business?

"Quit cryin' like a little girl. No way she heard a damned thing all the way upstairs, not with this storm. Besides, people with alarms get to countin' on 'em, you know?"

"Maybe for good reason. How do you know there's not a silent backup callin' the cops while we're here lookin'?"

"Not on these old-school systems. Don't worry, the thing's knocked out, all right. And if she hears anything, she'll just chalk it up to the rain."

"All the money in the world's no good if we end up busted, or maybe even in the ground."

"Listen, man. You wanna take your chances on your own, you can hotwire one of those trucks out there and take off, drive straight home to Mexico for all I care. But that money's my ticket to a new life. I'm not goin' anywhere without it."

Mac's money, Jake guessed. Had he stashed the missing millions here and told his fellow prisoners about it?

"What if it ain't still here? What if that bastard lied about it in the first place, or maybe slipped away and beat us to it? After all, this is his turf."

"Bullshit. He's a dead man. No way he got out of that fire alive."

"He'll kill us if he catches us here. Hell, crazy as he was, maybe his ghost will chase us down and—"

"You want to waste time jawin' about boogie men or you want to help me find that money?"

"It ain't in here, *hermano,* and we already know he didn't hide it in the stable or any of the cabins."

So, Jake thought, he had these two—or at least one of them—to thank for wrecking his place. Tempted as he was to burst into the room and give them the shock of their lives, he owed Liane a warning. He edged behind the entertainment center, then set the .38 on one of the shelves. After pulling out his cell phone, he punched in a quick text.

CALL SHERIFF. 2 MEN IN STUDY AFTER MONEY. OTHER ESCAPED CONS?

As soon as he hit Send he picked up the gun and moved back toward the study.

"Time to head upstairs, then," the deep-voiced man told his partner. "Might be the old man stashed it upstairs. Maybe in his bedroom. Mac's ex'll know."

The words chilled Jake to the marrow. *I'll shoot both of you dead before you take your first step up that staircase.*

"What if she's got a gun?" the Mexican asked.

"We catch her while she's sleeping, she won't have time to do a thing."

"You're one crazy *gringo.*"

"Crazy smart, 'cause you can bet your ass she knows something. If the old man had a safe, she'll have the combination."

"What if she won't tell us?"

"She'll tell us quick enough," the deep-voiced man said darkly. "All I have to do is shove my gun in her face."

"I thought you said you'd never hurt no woman."

There was a moment's hesitation before the man answered. "McCleary promised us a split. He *promised.* Besides, you know damn well that if they catch us, they won't bother takin' us back in. They'll shoot us down like damned dogs, so we got nothing to lose."

"Well, here's what I know, *hombre*. I been eight years in that hellhole, and I could seriously use a woman. So if you want somebody to put the fear of *Jesús* in her—and a little somethin' extra—I'm volunteerin' for the job."

Jake had heard enough. He surged forward, his gun in hand as he put his faith in his prosthesis and kicked the door wide open. Harnessing his anger, he ordered, "Drop your guns and raise your hands, or both of you are dead men!"

With the element of surprise on his side, his gambit should have worked. It might have, except he realized he'd made one crucial error.

A mistake that had him backpedaling and then diving for cover.

Chapter 10

Seconds after Liane received the text from Jake, she paced the room as she phoned for help, her fingers fumbling so badly that she had to redial twice.

Finally she was rewarded with a female voice saying, "Cascade County 9-1-1. What is your emergency?"

Panic throbbing in her chest, she whispered urgently, "There are strangers downstairs—inside my house! Send a deputy, please. I'm upstairs with my two kids."

"If you can give me your location," the dispatcher told her, "I'll send units out right away."

As Liane rattled off the address, then added her cell phone number in case they were cut off, she dragged her gaze from the locked bedroom door, where the dog stood whining, and saw that Cody was awake. His huge brown eyes were focused on her, then moved to the shotgun she was holding. She hurried over to him, knowing he must be remembering his grandfather's murder—and the night his father had tracked them down and kicked in the door to their hotel room. The night he'd shot her down.

This time, she vowed silently, *the story's going to have a different ending.* This time, if she was threatened, she had something a lot stronger than tears and pleas on her side.

For her children's sake, she would find the courage to pull the trigger. For her father's, she would pull a second time—blasting the intruders with both barrels.

Kenzie, too, was stirring now, but before she could ask questions, Cody whispered something to her and took her hand in his.

A loud bang from downstairs made all three of them jump. It was quickly followed by two others.

"Jake…" Liane moaned, before begging the dispatcher, "Please hurry! There's shooting, and my—my friend is down there."

Please, no, God, she prayed. *Please don't make me bury Jake, too.*

"Don't hang up," the dispatcher urged as Cody cried, "Where's Mr. Jake?"

Liane didn't disconnect, but she laid the phone down and pulled her children closer, shifting the shotgun to her other hand to touch each frightened face in turn.

They all flinched at the sound of angry voices downstairs, followed by another shot. A louder shout soon echoed up the stairwell. Liane quickly switched the gun back to her shooting hand.

With a whine, the normally intrepid Misty gave up her role as fierce protector to tuck her tail between her legs and run back to the bed.

"He's hurting Mr. Jake!" Cody cried, as the whining dog tried to force her too-tall body underneath the bed frame. "We have to go help him."

Pulse throbbing in her throat, Liane said, "No, Cody. He wanted us to stay here."

But as both her children wept, her mind catapulted back to last time. Though Kenzie had been too young to remember, her son knew, as she did, that huddling in the darkness and waiting like mice for help had not been enough to guarantee their safety. And that had been in Las Vegas, where the police had been less than ten minutes away, not the eternity it might take a deputy to get here.

Agony exploded low in her abdomen, the ghost of the gunshot that had cost her so much. Even worse than the resurrected pain was the memory of how utterly helpless she had been to protect her children that night. How could she, when she couldn't even keep herself safe?

But I didn't have a shotgun then. And I didn't have the courage.

Her father had, but he was dead now, taken from her by the same man who had robbed her of so much. Jake, too, had insisted on protecting her and her kids, and for all she knew he might be dead or dying, too, while she sat here doing nothing to help either of them, nothing to keep the violence from coming up the stairs and making its way into this room.

She looked down at Cody, seeing him through tears. "I need you to keep Misty here and lock the door behind me. Then you need to take Kenzie and hide in the closet, way in the back behind the clothes. Keep my phone and keep talking to the dispatcher. Anything she tells you to do, you do."

"I'm scared, Mommy," Kenzie said, reaching to clutch Liane around the waist. "Don't go."

Outside, wind-driven sheets of rain heightened their assault against the cabin's weathered exterior, as if the storm meant to wash away even the memory of the drought.

"It's okay, baby. I promise I'll be right back," Liane said soothingly, despite her mounting fear that she was making the wrong decision. But in the back of her mind she remembered how, on that night in Las Vegas, Mac had spent his fury on her, ignoring the children altogether. Though she had every intention of coming out of this alive, she would die willingly if that would spare her kids.

It was Cody who pulled his sister away. "Shh. You have to listen," he told her, sounding braver and more grown up than any eight-year-old should ever have to be.

Liane had never been prouder of both of them in her life.

"Don't open this door for anybody," she told them. "Nobody except me or Mr. Jake or a deputy."

While Kenzie sobbed, Cody nodded gravely and draped his arm around his sister's shoulder.

"I love you both," Liane told them, hating herself for leaving them, but hating even more the idea of waiting up here passively and making the room where she was holed up with her children ground zero in this fight. "Now, don't forget to lock up."

Because whatever had to happen, she decided, she was going to make sure it took place downstairs. She was going to do whatever it took to get the kids, herself and the man who had gone downstairs to protect them out of this alive.

Jake's thighs were cramping as he squatted behind the kitchen counter, but he didn't dare stretch.

Though he had meant to shock the two men as they argued, he had been the one surprised by the presence of a silent third person, a hook-nosed man with a scowl engraved into his long face.

And he was holding a revolver and covering the study door.

Both of them had fired so quickly that Jake had no idea

who had pulled the trigger first. Or how he'd survived to get off a second shot even as he leaped to one side and scrambled to safety.

His hearing sharpened by adrenaline, he made out, beyond the pelleting rain, a heavy thud that might have been the gunman's body falling. It was quickly followed by the rushing of two men leaving the room, one moving to the left, the other right.

Coming from a lit room into darkness, they would be temporarily blinded as their eyes adjusted, giving him a brief advantage. But now, with each rumble of thunder, lightning shone through the big windows, leveling the playing field.

"We've got you in our sights, so drop the gun and we'll spare the woman and her two brats," a deep voice boomed from his left. "Raise your hands and give up now, and you got my word we won't even touch her."

Jake knew better than to trust any promise made by an escaped fugitive intent on stealing a fortune. He was willing to bet the man was a liar, too. His instincts told him the guy had no idea where he was.

The intruder's words helped Jake pinpoint his location, but he couldn't get a clear shot into the living room without breaking cover, and he had no idea where the Mexican had gone.

Out the back door, Jake prayed, hoping the man valued his own survival more than money. But now that he had taken out one of their number—at least he prayed he had—the remaining cons might be too enraged to bail. And the Mexican might be too eager for a chance at the rape he'd threatened earlier. *I'll be damned if I let you lay a finger on Liane.*

The wind outside must have shifted, flinging raindrops hard as pennies into the glass. But Jake made out another sound behind him—the quiet sound of footsteps coming from behind.

Pulse thundering in his ears, he whipped around to face the threat.

As fast as he was, he was barely in time to see the muzzle flash.

Chapter 11

When the phone first started ringing, Sheriff Harry Wallace was having the dream again, the one where he was struggling out of the thick underbrush where he had been lost. Struggling from the shadows into bright light, only to encounter an undiscovered inland sea. Hot and breathless from his hike, he wanted more than anything to soak his tired feet, but the water churned and swirled, its slashing waves brown, and he knew instinctively that it was far too salty too drink. So salty, in fact, that it had poisoned every living thing that once made a home in and around it.

Still, his sore feet and his parched throat propelled him forward, no matter how hard he fought to stop himself.

Deke Mason's hand was just emerging from the waves and reaching toward him—pointing at him—when he felt his wife, Myrtle, shaking him awake. Starting upright, he stared at the empty bed beside him—empty since her death six months before.

She might be gone, as Deke was, but Myrtle was never truly absent. Even now, an echo of her voice urged, "Hurry up and get that, will you?"

Stomach burning, he snatched up the receiver and glanced at the clock. Unable to make out the fuzzy numbers, he fumbled for his glasses, noticing the heavy patter of the long-overdue rain. But it was the thunder and the wind that bothered him most, reminding him too sharply of the night his oldest friend had died.

"Wallace here," he huffed into the receiver.

"I don't know what I did, Uncle Harry," his grandniece wailed. "I must've hit the wrong button, and now I've cut him off! I've got a deputy heading out now, but what if it's too late?"

Harry sighed and rubbed his sternum, which still burned with the aftermath of the take-out burger he'd picked up on the way home. He should have known that punishing Camille by forcing her to work the night shift in dispatch would only come back to haunt him. Should have guessed that somehow she would manage to foul things up there, too.

"Cut *who* off?" he demanded as the clock came into focus. Two forty-three.

"The little Mason boy," Camille said. "He was hiding in the closet while his mother—"

"Cody Mason? What the hell is going on?"

"I tried to call him back, but—"

"Damn it, Camille," he said, already groping for his clothing. "Just explain from the beginning."

A ghost woven out of memory, his wife emerged from the pillows to sit up and stare at him—possibly out of concern that he was going to stir the whole family into a state by strangling his sister's granddaughter, if Camille's incompetence didn't end up giving him a stroke first.

As Camille filled him in on Liane's call, he switched on the lamp and Myrtle vanished. "Who's en route?" he asked.

"Winslow, sir. But he's still fifteen or twenty minutes out. He was all the way over in—"

"Who else?" he asked, reaching for his pants.

"That's it for now. Jackson's dealing with a domestic— that horrible Tyler Blake's gone and fallen off the wagon and—"

"I don't give a damn about that drunk. Get me every unit we have out there, and I'm heading that way, too."

From this side of Mill Falls, he might even beat his own men out there. But no matter how fast he drove, he was terrified that he wouldn't be in time.

Liane had been two steps down the staircase when she thought of Cody's bedroom and how ridiculous her father had thought she was for purchasing an emergency escape ladder to give the family an alternate escape route just in case.

She'd been imagining a house fire, not a break-in, when she'd bought it in response to her counselor's urging to deal proactively with any realistic terrors. But as she stood, poised to descend into the darkness, she couldn't move for worrying that whoever was down there would be expecting her to come this way.

So don't, then, she told herself, turning and racing for Cody's bedroom, then finding the package that contained the rope ladder and the red metal "arms" that grasped the sill. After tearing off her bulky robe, she shoved Cody's toy box out of the way and opened the window. A gust of wind sprayed her with cold rain that soaked through the thin cotton of her pajamas.

She told herself it didn't matter, that nothing mattered

except climbing down safely. Once outside, she could round the house and find or force her way inside.

Whatever you do, hurry! her own panicked voice screamed inside her head. *Hurry before they kill Jake— or come upstairs for the children!*

After positioning the red metal arms over the sill, she quickly stepped out of the window, though she felt awkwardly unbalanced with the shotgun under her arm.

Too awkwardly, it turned out, or else she'd been in such a panic that she hadn't correctly set the arms. Whatever the case, she'd barely started down into the wind and rain-whipped blackness when she found herself flipping backward.

She cried out, her arms windmilling as her right leg slipped through and hooked a ladder rung, jerking her to a graceless stop as the shotgun plunked down on the pine needles below. When she could breathe again, she realized she was dangling upside down, at least ten feet above the ground.

Her racing heart was stuffed somewhere in her throat. Would she fall and break her neck? Or had the intruders heard her? Paralyzed with terror, she cursed herself. She should have stayed back in the room like the little mouse she was.

"No," she said through gritted teeth as she grabbed another rung and fought to right herself. She hadn't been wrong to try to save Jake, herself and, most of all, her kids.

She would only be wrong if she gave up on saving the people she loved most in all the world.

Pain screamed along Jake's upper right arm, but somehow he managed to squeeze the trigger twice before rising. Shoving the injury out of his mind, he raced from his now compromised position, desperate to evade whoever had come up behind him.

Adrenaline gave him the strength to make his way back toward the staircase, that and his determination to buy Liane and the children enough time for the sheriff's deputies to arrive, even at the cost of his own life.

Fully expecting to be taken out at any moment, he clung to the deepest pools of shadow, crouching in frozen silence whenever lightning flickered and moving only when the room once more went dark. At some point he stopped hearing the rain and thunder, stopped noticing the pain, as his entire focus shrank down to the necessity of gaining another foot, a few more inches…a final chance to make his life count for something.

Finally he reached a point where no more cover was available. Forced to creep past the huge picture window that looked out across the black expanse of forest, he could only pray that another flash would not betray him.

He had nearly made it when the booming baritone finally broke the silence, and it came from far too close. "Drop the gun now or I pull this trigger. And believe me when I tell you, I don't miss from this distance."

"You got him, Smash?" Jake recognized the heavily accented voice. "Damned *cabrón* almost took my head off with that last shot!"

Footsteps approached, and then Jake felt the barrel of a gun jabbing into his back.

"You gonna drop that weapon," bellowed the deep-voiced man, "or am I gonna have to drop you?"

Straightening his back, Jake let his .38 clatter to the floor as the pain in his arm reawakened. "Sheriff's department's on the way," he warned the two men.

"Don't worry. You'll be dead before they ever get

here. Unless you tell us where that money is, or make that woman of yours—"

Jake's eyes slammed shut reflexively as someone switched a light on. It must have been the Mexican, because an instant later he was shouting, "*Mira!* She's outside!"

A shattering boom followed as the window glass exploded. Jake instinctively twisted, desperate to reach his gun before the huge man behind him fired.

Chapter 12

The moment the light came on, Liane looked inside and saw the gun pressed into Jake's back. She saw, too, the blood that soaked his sleeve and the defiant set of his jaw, the way his muscles coiled as he readied himself for what could only be a futile fight against the giant of a man behind him.

The need to help him surged through her veins like burning jet fuel. But before she could raise the shotgun to her shoulder, an ugly, dark-haired man with a gold front tooth shouted, aiming his gun toward her. Certain she was about to die, she shrieked, her finger contracting on the trigger.

A blast ripped the night in two, and something struck her squarely in the face. Gasping at the pain, she lost a stunned moment believing that she'd been shot before she realized that, with no time to brace herself against the recoil, her own gun had kicked back and dealt her a bruising blow.

Scrambling to recover, she looked back into the house. But the room had gone pitch-black again, leaving her with no idea whether the man she'd shot at was still a threat or where Jake had gone—or even if he'd been killed. Aware that she still had a second loaded barrel, she strained her ears toward the sound of something—some*one?*—being knocked to the floor. Was that fighting she was hearing? With fat raindrops popping all around her, she had no way of being certain, much less of pinpointing the disturbance.

A flash of red gave her hope—emergency lights rolling toward her down the long drive. Thinking only to flag down help, she spun toward the headlights—and what she prayed would be salvation.

But she hadn't made it three steps before she heard the pounding of fast-approaching footsteps just behind her.

Whipping around, she saw that a man with a gold tooth was nearly on her, bloody spots peppering his face and shirt. "You think you can get away with shooting at me, bitch?" he shouted, but he had to struggle to raise his weapon.

Pulse roaring in her ears, she used that split second to brace herself before the shotgun boomed in her hands. The man clutched at the huge new hole in his chest and folded in on himself, collapsing in the mud.

There was no motion, no sound, not even a groan. *Dead,* she thought numbly. She had killed a man.

"Liane, be careful!" someone called. *Harry!* She turned again and saw him rushing toward her as fast as his sixty-four-year-old legs could carry him. "He could still be—"

"Forget him." She said as she kicked the pistol away from the limp body. "We have to help Jake. He's inside with the other one. I saw them in the kitchen."

"You stay outside," he told her. "Or better yet, wait in my car where it's dry. And lock the doors."

She shook her head. "I can't," she said, though her teeth chattered and her legs threatened to give out. "My children are upstairs, hiding in a closet."

"Get in the damned car, Liane," he said sternly. "Or I swear I'm gonna cuff you and put you there myself."

Stunned into compliance, she did as she was told and was grateful to see a second department vehicle pull up beside the sheriff's. When the deputy bailed out, she lowered the window slightly and heard Harry tell him, "We've got at least one more intruder in the house, along with Jake Whittaker, and there are two kids hiding in an upstairs closet."

"That's one of the escapees," the deputy said as his flashlight skimmed the body. "I recognize his face."

After that they moved away, leaving Liane with no company except her own terror. Shaking worse than ever, she strained her ears and prayed she wouldn't hear more shots.

For the next few minutes—minutes that seemed to stretch into an eternity—she heard nothing, until the deputy came outside, trotting back toward her through the slackening rain. When he paused to check the man she'd shot for any signs of life, she climbed out of the car.

"Where are my children? Please, what's going on?"

"Sheriff wants you to come inside now," he said. "We found another intruder dead in the study, but it looks like the third one escaped out the back. We've got more deputies on the way to help track him down, but for the time being, you'll be safer—"

"Are my kids all right?"

"Your kids are fine—Sheriff Wallace just wants to talk to them for a minute before you come up." A brief smile quirked his thin lips. "Now that he's convinced your son to open the door for him."

She released the breath she had been holding. "What about Jake? He was bleeding—I saw it."

"Bullet cut across his arm. There's an ambulance on the way, but it doesn't look too serious. He was up and talking 'til the sheriff ordered him to settle down."

"Thank God," she said, breaking into a run. Because she had to see him for herself, to hold the solid warmth of his breathing body close to hers. When she'd glimpsed him through the window with those two men, she'd been scared to death that she would lose him.

Lose him? The irony of the idea struck her hard, since once upon a time she'd been too excited by the offer of a full scholarship, too certain her path lay elsewhere, to tie herself down with a boy she could never imagine living anywhere but the backcountry. But now that tragedy had tempered her view and she'd seen the value of the man she'd so carelessly walked away from, there was no way she could saddle him with a woman with her problems…a woman who could never give him the one thing he wanted and deserved.

The minute Jake saw her enter the kitchen, he rose from the chair where Harry had ordered him to wait. His lungs filled fully at the sight of her. She was a soaked, muddy, wild-eyed mess, but at least she looked to be in one piece. "Are you all right?" he asked, holding a towel against his bleeding arm. "I was so worried that guy would catch you."

"Oh, he caught her all right." Deputy Winslow gave what looked like an admiring smile. "Right before she blew a hole in his chest that you could pass an arm through."

Liane shivered, her teeth chattering audibly and her face as pale as moonlight. Before Jake could say a word, she was leaning against his chest and whispering, "You're bleeding."

And you're *in shock,* he thought, feeling like a heel for noticing the way her wet pajamas clung to those gorgeous curves of hers. She was soaking his sweatshirt, too, but he didn't care about that. Didn't care about anything except keeping her safe.

"I'll be fine. Are you okay?" he asked, wincing when she shifted, jostling his injured arm.

When she didn't answer, he wondered if she'd heard him. But she was so close that he felt her nod.

As Winslow draped a towel over her shoulders, she murmured, "Have to go get the kids. They'll be so scared. I…"

From upstairs, Harry called, "Liane, can you come on up? I've got a couple young folks here who're eager to see you."

She pulled away, staggering a few steps before Jake noticed the reddened spot on her cheekbone. "You *are* hurt," he said. "Let me help you."

"I'm fine," she assured him.

"You stay right here like the sheriff told you," Deputy Winslow ordered Jake. "I'll see Ms. Mason upstairs."

His arm throbbing, Jake relented. A few minutes later Harry came back downstairs alone.

"Thought it might be better to leave Liane up there with the children," he said. "There's no need for them to see the dead men, and I can always get her account of all this after you and I talk."

"Are the kids all right?"

"Shaken up, but they've got each other. And Liane's a good mama. She'll settle 'em right down."

But who would comfort *her*? Jake swallowed painfully, reminding himself that staying in the house for a few days and helping her with the aftermath of her father's murder hadn't made him a real part of her family. He'd been fooling himself, imagining he belonged here. Pretending that the kiss they'd shared was something more than a woman desperately trying to cope with grief.

"You hanging in there all right, Jake? You're looking a little rough."

"I've been worse," he reminded the older man as he continued applying direct pressure to the wound. Fortunately the bleeding had slowed down to a trickle. "I wouldn't recommend this, though. Hurts like hell."

"I'd call you a liar if you said any different. Paramedics shouldn't be much longer. We're gonna need to talk some more about how that dead fella ended up in the study."

"It's a real short story," Jake said impatiently. "When I ordered them to freeze, he fired at me. He missed. I didn't."

"I'll want the details later, but right now," Harry said, "I need to know more about the big fellow you said got away."

"After Liane shot out the window, that son of a bitch knocked me off my feet like a charging bull and sent my gun flying. Then he pointed his weapon at my face and…" Jake's mouth went bone dry as he relived the moment when his assailant's gun had clicked on an empty chamber. A moment when nothing but dumb luck—or the huge man's unwillingness to stick around to reload—had saved him. "I can hardly believe I'm here talking to you," he continued. "When he realized he was out of ammo, he ran for the back door. I would've tried to stop him, but…I guess I was a little stupefied to find myself still breathing."

Harry snorted. "You ought to be. You were one lucky son of a gun tonight."

"We'll drink to that," Jake told him, "soon as I get my drinking arm back in working order."

The sheriff smiled. "You better believe we will. Now, tell me everything you can remember about his appearance. I've already radioed for backup, but I'll need to call in a more detailed description for the highway patrol, the U.S. Marshals and whoever the hell else I can get out here."

"Bald, with a deep voice and muscles on top of muscles. Tattoos on his arms, maybe one on his neck, too."

"What kind of tattoos?"

Jake thought for a minute before shaking his head in frustration. "It was dark, and I was mostly focused on staying in one piece." Something else popped into his head, something from the convicts' conversation in the office. "I do remember the guy with the Mexican accent called him 'Smash.' Does that mean anything to you?"

Harry nodded. "Confirms what I've been thinking, that you just survived a run-in with an escaped con name of Herbert Newell, who's serving a forty-year sentence for three drug-related murders."

"His real name's *Herbert?*" Jake asked, incredulous.

Harry tilted another smile. "What d'ya want to bet he got the handle Smash from what he did to any idiot dumb enough to call him by his given name?" Sobering, he added, "You remember anything else they might've said? Anything about why they came?"

"They were definitely here looking for Mac's money."

"Mac's firm's money, you mean. Every bit of it conned out of unsuspecting investors." Harry rubbed at the frown lines creasing his forehead. "So the sneaking SOB hid it here, thinking he could come back for it later."

"From what I overheard," Jake said, "that's exactly what he did. Apparently he promised each man a cut in return for helping him, but the stash wasn't where he claimed he'd hidden it. They'd already checked out all the cabins and torn through the only one that wasn't empty."

"So that's who trashed your place." Harry shook his

head. "But what I want to know is where the hell's Mc-Cleary?"

"Burned to death out in the canyon, or at least that's what they figured." Jake shook his head. "I still can't imagine any way he could've made it out of there on his own, blinded the way he was. In that terrain, searchers could've missed the body, or it could've been burned to the point there wasn't much left to find."

"Well, turns out those hikers are still missing, so somebody took their car. Somebody smart enough to lay low—or get the hell out of Dodge before his partners caught up to him."

Harry nodded, then glanced out the broken window. "That ambulance is sure as hell taking its sweet time."

"I'm worried about Liane," Jake said. "She's the one who needs to be checked out. For shock, if nothing else."

"I'll see to it."

"And it's definitely not safe for her to stay here."

"Nobody's safe here right now. Do you think she's got a friend she and the kids can stay with for a spell?"

"I'm sure Em'll have room for them up at the lodge, but she won't want to leave the animals. I'll stay on."

Harry shook his head. "I don't like it one bit, especially since I don't have the manpower to leave a deputy here to stand guard."

"She won't go otherwise. And she has to. Don't worry about me. Once I'm patched up, I'll be fine. I'll keep a weapon on me, and Misty'll help keep watch."

"You're sounding awful cocky for a fellow with a black eye and a fresh bullet wound."

In spite of Harry's words, Jake saw nothing but approval in his gaze.

"Deke would be real pleased, seeing the way you've stepped up for her and the kids," the sheriff told him.

At the thought of his old friend, Jake felt his gut churn. "Do you really think he could've found the money Mac stole and kept it?"

Harry looked away, shaking his head. "He had plenty of opportunity to find it, and Lord only knows he had the motive. This place meant everything to him, and his bank accounts are all but empty. Have been for a good long while, yet somehow he'd been managing to keep things going. But his tax bill was paid just last week. Cash stuffed in an envelope—the whole year's worth at once."

"Maybe he sold off some other property or had another account somewhere."

"Listen, Jake, I want to believe he was innocent as much as anybody."

"It's not about what *we* want," Jake insisted. "It's about Liane and the kids. They've already been through so much. It would kill her to think her dad would—"

"I'm going to have to serve her with a warrant to search the premises."

"Just tell her you're looking for whatever Mac hid, not evidence against the man we just buried. Spare her the worry that she's about to lose her home."

"Even if it's true? Because if the FBI or the SEC figures out Deke was financing this place with stolen money, then I'm afraid there's nothing we can do to stop—"

Jake shook his head. "I'm not asking for forever. I'm just asking you to get solid evidence before you say anything to her about it. Can you do that?"

"I suppose I can. But you should know, I've already put a call in to the agent who's taken over the investigation into that crooked firm McCleary worked for. Haven't heard back yet, but I imagine we'll have federal company down here any day now."

"What if the money turned up sooner?" Jake asked. "If

someone found it where it couldn't possibly be connected to Deke Mason?"

Harry gave him a hard look. "You wouldn't be considering anything foolish, would you, Jake? Not to mention illegal."

"Of course not," Jake lied, already mentally sifting through strategies to find and move the missing money.

"And there's not something you're holding back? Something you might know?"

"Deke never said a word to me about Mac McCleary or any missing money."

"Then stay out of this, you hear me? Deke wouldn't have wanted to see you get in trouble, and that goes double for me."

Instead of answering, Jake glanced toward the stairwell. "Like I said before, this isn't about me."

Catching his meaning, Harry sighed. "You know, we might not be doing her any favors, keeping this back. Once she hears I'm digging into Deke's finances, it won't be pretty."

"You have enough on your plate," Jake told him. "Just let me worry about Liane for now."

Chapter 13

"I hate this," Liane told Em four days later, as they left the crowded parking lot of the elementary school. It was the first time she'd left Cody and Kenzie out of her sight since the break-in, a thought that prompted a flutter of panic in her stomach.

Em, who was driving a shiny white Range Rover with the Wolf River Lodge & Spa logo emblazoned on each side, smiled reassuringly. "Look, you were the one who told me you wanted them to get back to a normal routine as soon as possible. And what could be more normal than the first day of school?"

"I know that. And I know that getting back to work in a few days is going to be a positive for me, too. But I can't help worrying."

"You've made the principal, their teachers and the school counselor aware of the situation. They've promised you that neither of the kids will be left unsupervised, that you'll have to come to the office and personally sign them out. And if any strange man shows up around campus, they'll call the sheriff's office immediately. And Sheriff Wallace himself came by yesterday to tell you that other convict was caught at a roadblock in a stolen car. He's locked up tight now, and your ex must have burned to a crisp, which would be poetic justice, if you ask me."

"What if he didn't? What if he's biding his time and—"

"You're obsessing again." Em slapped on the no-nonsense voice she normally reserved for the occasional drunken rowdy at the lodge's bar. "You asked me to tell you if you were, so I'm calling you on it."

Liane glared at Em—who was sounding more like her counselor than her best friend—for a moment before blowing out a breath. "You're right. I'm obsessing. I've done everything possible already, so this garbage isn't helping. It's high time to move the kids back home and figure out our future. Otherwise, I'm letting Mac win."

Em imitated the bright dinging of a slot machine paying out. "You just won the grand prize! Breakfast out at Toni's. I seem to remember you're a sucker for the apple-walnut waffles with whipped cream."

"Thanks, but I couldn't. My stomach's all in knots."

"Your stomach is rebelling because it's forgotten what food feels like. Haven't you noticed how loose your clothes are getting? You're making me look like a damned parade float standing next to you, and you know how I hate that."

Liane surprised herself by laughing. "Good to hear there's a little healthy self-interest buried in there somewhere. You've been so sweet and generous and patient lately, I was beginning to wonder if the pod people had replaced you."

Liane ended up agreeing to breakfast, mostly to repay her friend for being the best boss she could imagine, and before long Em's shameless flirting with the waiter had her blushing.

"Toni's going to ban you for life if she catches you hitting on her son like that," Liane whispered when the nineteen-year-old left their table, a big, loopy grin on his face.

Em waved off her misbehavior. "She knows I'm just playing."

"But does *he* think so?"

Em shrugged happily. "Oh, honey. Boys at that age never think. It's one of my most favorite things about them."

"One of these days someone's going to call your bluff, Em."

"Oh, I dearly hope so. And I hope it's a luscious fire-fighter this time."

Liane dropped her gaze to her coffee, reminded that one of the notches on Em's bedpost belonged to Jake Whittaker—and she was far more bothered by the fact than she liked to admit.

"Don't worry," Em said soothingly, as if she'd read Liane's discomfort. "If you're worried about me swooping in on Jake again, forget it. He's not my type, believe me."

Liane speared her with a look. "Since he lost his leg, you mean?"

Em set down her coffee cup and made a dismissive gesture. "You know darned well we broke up before he was hurt, so I won't dignify that with an answer. I *meant* since he made it clear that he's the type who plays for keeps."

"Jake?"

Em nodded. "We'd never even done the deed before I had his number."

Liane was overwhelmed by the sense of relief cascading through her. "You mean, you two never...?"

Em shook her head. "No way, not when it was so obvious that man was burned out on the game and looking for a wife. And, heaven help me, *babies*."

She made the sign of the cross, warding off the very notion. Great as she was with Liane's children, Em had insisted from the time they were in high school that she was cut out to be an eccentric aunt and not a mother.

Meanwhile, a lump formed in Liane's throat. She'd always known he wanted his own family, so why shouldn't he have started looking elsewhere after she'd turned him down? Still, the thought was so painful that pure contrariness had her saying, "For someone supposedly on the make for a wife and kids, he sure seems to spend a lot of time holed up in his cabin."

"Last summer had to be hard on him," Em allowed. "But I've been thinking there might be another reason he's been sticking close to home just lately." She raised her delicate brows and gave Liane a meaningful look.

Still thinking of Jake's gentle strength, of the kiss that had blazed up between them, Liane understood that Em was right, that the tragedy of her father's death had rekindled feelings on both their parts. But as true as their connection felt, she knew that the fair thing, the right thing, to do would be to distance herself from him instead of allowing both herself and her kids to grow any more dependent.

Because the Jake she'd come to know again, the man she couldn't help but care for, deserved a family, the kind that came with kids of his own. And even if she ever emotionally or financially recovered from this latest blow, that was something she could never give him—not since the emergency hysterectomy the surgeons had performed to save her life after the shooting.

Holding up her palms, she argued, "Jake's my father's

tenant. That's all. There's nothing more between us. Hasn't been for years."

Em scooted her chair back, its feet screeching against the tile.

"What's wrong?" Liane demanded, irrationally irritated by the way her friend had attracted the attention of half the cafe.

"I'm just moving out of range in case you're struck by lightning," Em said. "Because I'm pretty sure you've never told a bigger lie in all your life."

When her cell phone rang, Liane was packing up the suite she and the kids had been using, and wondering how long it would be before finances would force her to leave her father's place, too. Grateful for the distraction, she didn't even bother looking at the Caller ID window when she picked up.

"Hello?"

"Ms. Mason, this is Hal Shoemaker."

"Oh, hi, Hal," she said, recognizing the name of the local feed and tack store owner. Her father had done business with him for decades. "Before I forget, I wanted to say how good it was to see you and your wife at the funeral."

"It's a terrible thing. We all still can't believe it. I keep expecting your dad to call or walk in to look at the new saddles. My heart goes out to you and your family."

"Thank you," she said. "Is there something I can do for you?"

"Well, yes. I hate to bother you with this now—"

"I can't put off reality forever," she said, hoping that her already strained bank account wouldn't be hit too hard. "How much did my father owe you?"

"No, Liane. It's not that. Your father had a credit balance. I found an envelope with cash left on my desk one day. He'd not only taken care of his bill, he'd paid in advance for the next five months. I wasn't sure he'd mentioned it to you, and I thought you ought to know, since your dad mostly did business on a handshake. He was a good customer and a good man."

"You're saying he paid five months ahead in *cash?* When?"

"Last month. He paid off what he owed, plus another five months."

"How much?" she asked, her voice shaking. "How much did he give you?"

When Hal Shoemaker named the figure, what should have been good news crashed in on her like a wrecking ball. Because her father couldn't have come up with that much money. Not through any means she knew of.

After thanking Hal, she hung up, her mind desperately wheeling through the possibilities. Could her father have cashed in an insurance policy or taken out a loan against the property? Had she missed something, some resource she didn't know of?

But as desperately as she tried to come up with other explanations, she had a sinking feeling that she finally knew what Harry Wallace and his deputies were looking for in their third search of the property in as many days.

And she would be damned if she allowed him to turn her father, a murder victim, a man loved and respected by everyone, into some kind of criminal scapegoat for her ex-husband's crime.

After forcing open a kitchen window and slipping inside, the first thing Mac did was wolf down a pair of honey-glazed donuts from a box the homeowners had left on the counter. He washed down the lump of doughy sweetness with the still-warm dregs of a pot of coffee, and bitter as it was, he was so grateful that he could have wept for joy.

He'd just picked up the last donut in the box in his filthy, shaking hand when a bolt of panic stopped him. What the hell was he thinking, snatching food and drink from the counter, where they were sure to be missed, with no more thought than some half-starved animal? For the past week he'd played it smart, lying low in a shuttered old vacation cabin he'd found off a logging road miles from the fire. Though mice had destroyed what was left of an old sofa, and the roof was leaky, he'd found a cache of canned goods—much of it years past its expiration date—to supplement what he'd found in the hiker's backpack, along with the privacy he'd needed to heal from his scrapes, bruises and the racking cough he'd picked up from the smoke.

But far worse than the physical discomfort were the worries that gnawed at him. Had Liane, in her terror, led both his kids to their deaths? And if she'd died, too, had she taken with her his last hope for finding out what had happened to his money?

With no TV or newspapers, and not even a working radio in the hikers' ancient car, it had been his desperation to find out that had finally forced him to risk traveling again, using back roads to thread his way toward the one place where he could find answers. But the closer he'd gotten, the more he'd realized how naked and exposed he was without a weapon, so when he'd seen a pickup truck pull out of a driveway with an older couple inside, he'd decided to take a chance that, like most of the yahoos in this area, they had some sort of gun in the house to ward off troublesome wildlife.

As he walked through the family room, the sight of several mounted bucks' heads had him grinning in anticipation, and soon he was on his way, taking with him a pistol he had liberated from the back of a gun cabinet the homeowner had thoughtfully left unlocked.

As he walked to where he'd hidden his car behind a woodshed, he realized he had taken a huge risk, a foolish risk, choosing a house so close to the Mason ranch. Once his theft was discovered—and the homeowners could return at any moment—he had no doubt that law enforcement would swarm the area and maybe even bring in dogs to try to catch his scent.

So leave now. Get out while you still can....

But the thought of abandoning the money—money he'd accumulated through a canny combination of cunning, nerve and patience—stopped him in his tracks. He damned well *deserved* better from life than skulking like a stray dog and surviving on other people's leavings. It infuriated him to think of who he'd once been and all the hellish years he'd put in to achieve his success, years he'd spent convincing everyone from get-rich-quick schemers to large corporations' pension boards to invest.

Long before any of the others whom he worked with, he'd realized that his boss's whole elaborate strategy was nothing but a giant Ponzi scheme. At first he had thought of going to the authorities, until he'd realized that in doing so he would lose everything he'd worked for, from the Mercedes to the new house to the reputation that made people look up to him—including the beautiful young innocent he'd wanted from the first time he'd spoken to her.

Unable to bear the thought, he'd kept on working, skimming a little off the top to take care of his family. And why not? It wasn't as if any of those greedy and gullible investors were ever going to see their money again anyway, especially not after his boss had funneled off more than a hundred times what Mac had pilfered and disappeared once the FBI and SEC investigations had finally zeroed in on him.

In the end, however, it was the stolen car that made the decision for him when it stubbornly refused to start. Despite a desperate search of the property, Mac found no vehicle to steal to get him out of there.

So this was it, he realized. He had no choice but to walk to the Mason ranch. To take one last shot at reclaiming what had been taken from him.

And one last shot at paying back the woman who had never for a single moment appreciated that everything he'd done, he'd done to make the perfect life his family deserved.

As Jake stepped onto his front porch, Misty slipped out growling, the hackles on her back raised.

"Back inside," Jake ordered the dog, who gave one last rumble before tucking her tail between her legs and slinking back through the door. To Harry Wallace, he said, "Sorry. She's been a little on edge since Deke…"

"Can't say as I blame her." Harry's forehead creased with concern.

Noticing the dark circles shadowing the sheriff's eyes, Jake asked, "Are you doing all right, Harry? You didn't strain yourself digging for that money, did you?"

"That's why I hire young deputies," Harry countered with a smile that looked more like a grimace. "Don't you worry, I'll be all right. It's just been a lot of long hours lately, that and worrying over what the feds will find that I missed."

"Not to mention you lost a good friend last week. Your best friend."

Rather than replying, Harry abruptly changed the subject. "So how's the arm?"

"Not too bad, considering." With the sling more a hindrance than a help, Jake had downed a couple of ibuprofen and ditched it a few hours earlier.

Harry studied his face. "The eye looks a lot better, too. So how have things been out here?"

"Nice and quiet," Jake answered, though he'd been lying awake night after night, jumping up and reaching for his gun with every creak and crack in or near the cabin he'd spent his days setting back to rights.

Maybe it was the lack of sleep, or the pain from his gunshot wound, but sometimes it seemed as if Deke was at his side again, still talking about tools and foundations as the two of them planed the floor and sanded down the new cabinets they'd built for the galley-style kitchen.

"Just because the place is small," Deke had once told him, *"doesn't mean it shouldn't be every bit as solid as we can build it. Look at the homestead over there. You think my grandfather built it up to be a great big lodge like that? No, sir. He started out with a little place no bigger than this bunkhouse. As the children started coming, he and he sons built on all around and above it. But inside those old walls is the beating heart of everything my grandfather and his sons created, everything I have, you hear me? Even if I'm long gone, if all the rest burns down or blows away, it's the one place my family can always look to for their future."*

At the time Jake had only nodded, filing Deke's seemingly idle chatter away with all the other advice he had always been so eager to impart. But knowing what he knew now, Jake couldn't help but wonder what else the old man had been hinting at.

He knew he should mention it to Harry, to point him in the direction that had been taking shape in his mind ever since he remembered the conversation. But somehow he couldn't bring himself to say anything, not without first checking out his hunch himself—and thinking through how any discovery might impact Liane.

Harry released a sigh. "Can't say I haven't been a little worried, even with your buddy *Herbert* back in custody. But I guess I would've heard from you if there'd been any sign of trouble out here."

Jake offered a strained smile. "Right after I shot whatever it was dead, you would've been first on my list to call."

Harry smiled back and nodded. "Can't say I blame you. Listen, Jake. I want you to know that this is it for us. My deputies and I are turning the investigation over to the FBI this afternoon. They'll send a team to go over this place with a fine-tooth comb. And they have the resources to search for any additional assets or offshore accounts that might be involved."

"Then you really think Deke took that money?"

Harry shook his head. "At this point, I've got no idea. But I can tell you for certain, whatever Deke might've done, you can bet your life he did it for his family. Maybe he figured after everything Mac put Liane though, she deserved a secure home, at the very least."

Jake was inclined to agree, but he didn't imagine any judge would. "Have you told her yet?"

Harry shook his head. "I've been putting that part off, but I'm heading over to the lodge to try to catch her right now."

"I don't envy you that conversation," Jake said, "but once the Feds start digging, there won't be any keeping it from her anyway."

"Maybe they won't find anything, just like you said."

"I hope to God they don't," Jake said, "because the last thing Deke ever would've wanted is to see this place auctioned off to strangers."

As Harry prepared to leave, the two shook hands, and Jake couldn't help but notice that the sheriff wouldn't meet his eyes.

Jake knew that if he were caught, he would be arrested, that if he found anything at all and didn't immediately report it, he could be charged with obstructing an investigation, tampering with evidence, or maybe even theft. But with no one in sight, he shoved aside those worries and went to the tack room where Deke kept his tools.

He tucked a pair of work gloves into the back pocket of his jeans, then grabbed a hammer, a screwdriver, a pickax and a crowbar. About halfway to the homestead, he belatedly remembered the set of house keys Liane had left him. Cursing his forgetfulness, he turned back to his cabin, intent on grabbing them, then getting down to business.

But before he could leave, Misty pranced and yelped, air-kissing the door as she fanned her thick gray tail.

"Liane," he murmured, recognizing the greeting the dog reserved for family members. Cursing Liane's timing, he looked around the cabin for a place to stash the tools. Left with few options since his cleanup, he ducked behind the half wall obscuring this bedroom and had just shoved everything beneath the bed, hidden by the oversize fringed spread, when the knocking started.

"Just a second," he called, breathing hard as he rushed to the door. "Liane, what's going on?" he asked a moment later, taken aback to see her looking as furious as a shaken bag of bees. Could she have spotted him with the tools when she'd been driving up and jumped to the wrong conclusion?

Instead of hurling accusations, she fended off Misty's greeting and said, "I thought I'd catch Harry out here. When did he leave?"

So she was gunning for the sheriff. Jake wondered if she'd somehow figured out what Harry suspected her father of.

"You just missed him," Jake told her. "They didn't find a thing, though. He did tell me that much."

"If the money was ever really here in the first place, someone took it," she insisted, her eyes fierce and her color high. "Probably years ago. The ranch might not be what it once was, but there've been wranglers helping with the horses, part-time guides during the busy season. And we have guests here all the time. Any one of them could have gone poking around and come across it."

"You may be right," he said, needing to defuse her anger.

"It wasn't Dad," she insisted. "If he'd found it, he would have known it belonged to the investors and he would have returned it. My father wouldn't steal, Jake. He'd rather starve than do that."

Let her go find Harry, he told himself. *Let* him *break it to her.* But as much as he wanted to get inside the house to search what Deke had called its heart, he couldn't bear to let her leave here so upset. "Come on in. Please. Have some coffee. I just made a fresh pot."

She hesitated, one corner of her mouth quirking downward. "I should go," she said, frustration shimmering in her eyes. "I—I need to make the sheriff, need to make *all* of them, understand."

He should let her leave, he knew. But when a tear broke free, he couldn't stop himself from brushing it aside with his thumb.

She stiffened at the contact, a light flush coloring her

face. When her gaze dropped, he wondered if she was thinking of their kiss, too, and the fact that the two of them were alone together and only steps from his bed. Or had he only been imagining that she, too, felt the tidal pull of old attraction? That she was capable right now of feeling anything but grief?

"All I'm asking is for you to sit down so we can talk about it," he said. "*I'd* like to sit down, anyway. I've been working on this place for hours, and I—"

She winced, sounding instantly contrite as she looked to his sleeve, bulky with the bandages beneath it, and said, "I'm sorry, Jake. How are you? I should've started there."

"I won't lie and say the arm hasn't bothered me, but it seems to be healing well. Well enough that I've ditched the sling."

She nodded, relief smoothing her features as she stepped inside. "I'm so glad. What you did the other night…I can't begin to thank you."

"You thanked me at the E.R. There's no need to say any more about it."

"Of course there is. You risked your life for my family. And not for the first time." She touched his hand for a fleeting moment before pulling back abruptly, her gaze avoiding his.

"Have a seat, and let me get that coffee," he said, nodding toward the sofa. "It's not much to look at, but it beats standing."

"Nice repair job," she said, nodding toward the slashed cushions.

"You know what they say." He lifted two clean mugs— survivors of the wreckage—from their hooks and filled them with hot, strong coffee. "Necessity's the mother of duct tape. For now, at least, since a new laptop had to take priority over a new sofa."

"I hope you didn't lose too much work," she said.

"I back up my work daily to an online vault." Remembering how she liked her coffee, he stirred in a splash of milk before passing her the mug. "I've got a huge deadline only a few weeks away, so it's definitely saved my *bacon*."

Since the other chair had been damaged beyond redemption, he sat down next to her. He tried not to notice, not to mind, when she scooted away from him, perching on the edge of the cushions. He'd been right. She clearly regretted "forgetting herself" with him. She'd wanted nothing except a friendly port in one of the worst storms of her life.

"I can't believe Harry thinks my dad stole that money," she said, her eyes gleaming with emotion. "I thought he was worried about solving his murder, when all the time he's been out to destroy my father's good name—the only thing he has left."

"You're half right," Jake admitted. "Harry's been looking at that possibility. But it's not the only thing on his mind. Anyone can see it's tearing him apart, but it's his job to find out everything he can about why Mac wanted to hurt your father."

"Mac was furious when I testified against him. Forget the fact that he hurt me—"

"Shot you," Jake corrected.

Her eyes slid closed, and she swallowed hard. "He'd do anything to get back at me. He was obsessed with revenge."

"Liane, those men who came here—they were definitely after the money Mac took. Money he'd promised them if they would help him escape."

"He'd say anything to get to me," she insisted.

"Harry thinks that maybe—"

"What I can't understand is why Harry hasn't talked to *me* about his suspicions."

"Because I asked him not to," Jake admitted. "Not until he had proof."

Liane jumped up from the sofa. "You *what?* Why on earth would you do a thing like that?"

Realizing he'd said the wrong thing, he opted for the simplest, most honest explanation. "The night of the break-in, when Harry and I first discussed this, I couldn't bear to see you hurt any more."

She banged the mug down on the counter that separated the small kitchen from the living area. "I appreciate all your help, but I'm not a child. I don't need to be shielded from all the bad things in life."

He set his own cup on the floor and went to her, moving in too close. But he'd backed her against the counter, so she had nowhere to retreat. "No, you aren't a child, Liane. But that night, you had two scared kids to deal with, and you were in shock. You were cold and soaked and shaking, and you'd just been forced to kill a man."

"It's no more than you did, and you'd been shot, too," she said, her eyes blazing. "But no one assumed you were weak and in need of—"

"Believe me, no one who's seen the risks you've taken for your family's safety could ever think of you as weak. But being a fighter doesn't make you indestructible, and no matter how pissed you are at me for it, I'd do the same thing if I had it to do all over."

She thrust her chin toward him in a look of pure defiance. "Then why didn't you tell me later?"

"Don't you understand, Liane?" He leaned over her, so close that he saw everything from the dewy sheen of her skin to the way her pupils dilated at his nearness. "Because it's not in me to hurt you. Never has and never will be."

In the space of a few seconds the stone wall of her anger crumbled. Her shoulders sagged as sadness overtook her.

"Why, Jake," she asked quietly, regret shadowing each word, "when I know how much I've hurt you? How much my choices have hurt us both."

His heart bumped a quick warning, but it wasn't fast enough to stop the truth from slipping free. "It's because I love you, Liane. Always have and always will."

As he dipped his head closer still, she whispered, "It's not right. I—I can't do this."

But a few achingly long moments later she was the one who, with a soft cry of surrender, finally closed the space between them.

Chapter 14

It was so wrong of her to do this, to give in to her body's long untended needs, to her craving for the man who had first awakened her to passion. She would have stopped herself, would have forced herself to step back, but the things he had risked saying had shattered her defenses.

He still loves me, her mind sang as the heat and moisture of their kisses deepened. *Still wants me.*

I should tell him first. Tell him why we can never...

But the thought went up in flames as his fingertips slid along the curve of her neck and he dropped his mouth to tongue a blazing trail from the sensitive spot beneath her ear down to the hollow of her collarbone.

"Jake, please," she said, arching her neck as her legs gave in to trembling. "We need to..."

Her objections melted as his big hands pulled her closer, sending delicious chills rippling through her to squeeze into a tight ball of anticipation.

Her breasts ached for his touch, the nipples peaking with her need, but standing here against the counter felt so awkward. She caught his arm and whispered the only coherent words that came to mind. "The bed. Now."

He looked up, his brown eyes drugged not just with desire but the love that had always been there, if she'd only opened her eyes to it. In that moment she would have followed him anywhere, done absolutely anything he asked.

"You're sure?"

Unable to say more, she nodded, and he kissed her softly, deeply, driving her wild with the heat and moisture and slick thrust of his tongue. She was whimpering with need by the time he stopped to let the dog outside and then led her around the little half wall that shielded his freshly made bed from view.

When she sat down on the mattress and started to unbutton her blouse, he sat beside her and pushed her hands aside. "Let me. Please. I've waited so long for this. Imagined it so many times. Imagined *you*."

Her eyes filled as she thought about him out here by himself night after night, surrounded only by the darkness.

But his attention was riveted to his work, the task of undoing each small button, starting from the top. He sucked in a sharp breath at the sight of her cleavage.

"You've filled out some since I last saw you," he said appreciatively.

"Two babies will do things to a woman's body," she murmured, suddenly conscious of competing with his memories of her seventeen-year-old self.

He continued unbuttoning, dipping his mouth to kiss the plump, pale tops of her breasts. "You," he whispered, "have never been more beautiful."

She moaned, her restless fingers running through his

hair to pull him closer. Soon he had her shirt off, and with a deft flick of his wrist, the bra followed.

She thought she would fly apart the moment he laid her back and took one nipple into his mouth. The pleasure coiling beneath her belly tightened, pulsing urgently.

As he feasted on each breast in turn, she clawed at his T-shirt, until she finally pulled it over his head. Her jeans went next, in a fumbled hurry, with Jake kissing each inch of exposed flesh, his every movement driving her pulse faster.

When he hesitated, the memory of her scars hit her like a shower of ice water. Sure enough, when she looked down, she saw him studying the shiny knot of tissue and the incision line along her lower belly—an all-too-stark reminder of what had been taken from her.

"Don't look," she begged, moving to cover the ugliness with her hands. "Please."

He looked up, his eyes dark. "You never need to hide from me. I have scars of my own."

Her face was burning. "But it's so—it's repulsive."

"It's fine. I promise," he said, stroking her hand until she relaxed enough to gently move it aside. "And I want you to know, there's nothing about you I could ever find repulsive. Nothing."

"But he—because of him, I can never have more—" Pain shuttering her eyes, she shuddered, her flesh crawling at the memory of the doctor telling her about the extent of the damage.

"Shh, Liane. Just trust me, please. Believe me when I say I've never wanted you more than I do at this moment."

She wanted to deny him, to explain to him that he deserved far better. But she made the mistake of looking at him, her gaze slowly drifting from the sculpted perfection of his six-pack abs to the sheer masculine beauty of his lightly haired chest to the undeniable hunger in his eyes.

When was the last time anyone had looked at her that way?

Remembering the cave and that first time— both their first times—she swallowed hard, then answered his un-spoken question with the subtlest of nods. Judging from his smile, it was enough.

He caught the elastic edge of her bikini panties with one finger and ever so slowly eased them down until she stepped out of them, his gaze taking in every inch of her.

"So damned lovely," he whispered. "So very beautiful."

"You don't have to say that," she assured him, still too conscious of the damage to her body.

"Would you wait for me one minute?" he asked. "I'd like—it would be more comfortable if I take off my pros-thetic. If that's all right with you."

Swallowing hard, she nodded again, understanding that for him this moment must be even more difficult than it had been for her.

She tried to look away politely, not wanting to embar-rass him. But he said, "It's no big deal. See?" and showed her the way the leg came off, from rolling back the sili-cone sheath to removing what was left of his leg, which ended just below his knee, from the prosthetic's socket.

"Still with me?" he asked, a flicker of uncertainty in his eyes, as if he feared he might have gone too far. A flicker that reminded her of the vulnerable boy whom she had once loved. And the man? Did she still love the man?

When she finally found her voice again, she couldn't come up with the right words, so she borrowed those she needed. "Believe me when I say, Jake, I've never wanted you more than I do at this mom—"

He cut her off with a kiss, a kiss that pushed even the

memory of fear and pain and violence from her mind. Pushed aside everything but the desperate need to be touched and tasted and filled up by this man.

And as morning turned to afternoon, she took all that she needed and gave back even more.

Jake had lost track of how much time had passed when he felt her move away and get up, the abrupt absence of her soft curves setting off another wave of wanting. Though they'd already made love twice, he wasn't close to sated. Couldn't imagine ever having his fill of the woman he had waited half a lifetime to reclaim.

Reaching for her, he murmured, "Come here, you."

But she'd slipped out of range, and when he opened his eyes he saw that she was already dressed. She wasn't looking at him. Instead, she was staring at a point on the floor. At first he thought his prosthetic leg had captured her attention, but her widening eyes and growing pallor quickly convinced him otherwise.

"What on earth are those tools doing under your bed?" she asked, her voice growing frostier with every syllable, reminding him of the icy mask she'd hidden behind for so long.

For about a nanosecond he considered trying to convince her he'd been using them to get his cabin back in order. But he couldn't bring himself to lie to her, not after everything they'd shared. Besides, she would soon know more than enough to figure out that he hoped to find the missing money before the FBI did, and he couldn't live with the risk that she would suspect he'd meant to keep it for himself.

"After Harry spoke to me," he admitted, sitting up with the sheet pooled in his lap, "I remembered something.

Something your dad once said to me that made me wonder if—"

"Then you believe it, too." Her eyes glittered, as frozen as her voice. Frozen as if her long thaw in his arms had been no more than a false spring. "You think my father was a thief."

"Your father didn't steal that money. Mac did."

"My father knew that people, innocent investors, lost their savings, their retirement. If he'd found a dime of it, he would have turned it in."

"He talked about the homestead, about the cabin it was built around. I only remembered this morning how he said that foundation would keep his family secure long after he was gone."

"So why didn't you tell Harry?"

"Because I didn't want him to find it," he admitted.

She turned away from him, deftly pulling back her long hair and banding it in a loose ponytail.

"If your father really found the money and hid it there, I didn't want you—or anyone—to know," he told her.

Her shoulders stiffened. "You would have kept it from me?"

"I thought I would. Thought I might try to move it someplace where it would be found but not connected with your father."

Slowly she turned back to face him. "Mac kept me in the dark about his business—about everything. And you know how that turned out."

"So you're comparing me to *him* now?" Jake felt a rush of heat as his anger flared to life. "A man who kept secrets to protect himself, never you? A man who beat you, shot you, killed your father, when I've never done a damned thing except—"

Except love you, he'd been about to say, and, though

it was the truth and nothing he hadn't already said, he couldn't get the words past the knot of old resentment.

"Of course you're not like him. If you were, do you think I ever would have…?" Shaking her head, she changed the subject, ignoring her phone, which suddenly began to ring. "The point is, I won't be lied to. Not by anybody, not even to protect me."

"All right, then. Admit the truth," he challenged. "Your father could have found that money, could have talked himself into thinking it was the right thing to use it to save the ranch for you and the kids."

"I'll believe it when you prove it."

"Then come with me," he told her. "Let's go up to the homestead and find out if I'm right."

Harry put the phone down and wondered where the hell Liane was. It wasn't like her not to answer, and when he'd tried the lodge, a desk clerk had told him she was nowhere on the premises.

He had to find her before some FBI suit showed up to blindside her. As Deke's best friend, he owed her the truth, no matter how painful.

Camille stuck her head into Harry's office. "Could I maybe bring you some more coffee?"

She sounded tense, as if she expected him to light into her again at any moment. Though it was no more than she deserved, he didn't have the heart for it, so instead he waved her in and said, "No coffee, thanks, Camille, but come on in, why don't you? It's high time you and I had ourselves a little talk."

She nodded as she crept inside on mouse feet.

"Have a seat," he invited, nodding to the chair in front of his desk.

She shook her head, then took a deep breath and braced herself. "I think I'd rather stand for this."

So she knew. Well, that was better. These things were a lot harder when the other person was surprised. Though his sister would make his life hell for doing a thing like this to her "grandbaby," Camille was still young. Young enough that a dismissal from this dead-end job, along with last-week's breakup with her dead-end boyfriend, might be exactly what she needed to get her to take another stab at finishing her schooling.

Bracing himself for the hard part, he dropped his bottle of antacids back into his desk drawer.

"Before you get started, though," she blurted, passing him a sheet of paper, "you'll probably want to see this email from Special Agent Davies about what she'll need to facilitate her investigation. I've highlighted all the need-to-know stuff."

"So Harper Davies is a woman?" Harry asked, not wanting to embarrass himself with a gaffe. "You're sure?"

"Definitely." Camille's voice grew steadier as she continued. "We talked for quite a while earlier. She sounded young. And she was so *nice*."

"You talked?" As Harry dug through the stack of memos, reports and other papers littering his desk, he swore he could feel his blood pressure rising. "You forget to take the message?" *Again*.

"Oh, there was no message," she hastened to assure him. "She just wanted to get to know a little about the department and the people she'd be interacting with here."

"The people?" Over the course of his long career he'd run across—and been forced to cooperate with—FBI agents now and again, but he'd never met one who'd acted halfway interested in finding out about the local law enforcement team, unless… Did they suspect him of incompetence? Or worse?

"Sure," said Camille. "Like you, for instance. She had a lot of questions about you."

Alarm jolted through him. What the hell?

"You know," Camille elaborated. "The way you run things, what you're like to work with, that sort of thing." With a shrug, she added, "The little quirks that make you special."

Harry didn't like it any more than he liked the shrewd sparkle replacing Camille's blush. She darned well *knew* she'd snagged his full attention, and she was enjoying his discomfort. "So what exactly did you tell the *nice agent,* Camille?"

She smiled—the first real smile he'd seen from her in days. Yep. The kid was definitely having fun here in what she clearly suspected were her final moments on the job. That, in combination with her ability to coax some sort of sense from the machines he was forced to deal with more and more often lately, convinced him she was a lot sharper than her recent screw-ups would suggest.

Sharp enough to warrant one more chance, he decided when she left him hanging.

"Would it help to know you're not getting fired?" he asked. *Not today, at any rate.*

"Really? That's so awesome. Because I have some ideas—ways to help streamline things around here, get rid of all this old-school paper you have cluttering your office and—"

"Let's not get carried away. Now tell me, before I drag you into the interrogation room and break out the rubber hoses, what exactly did you tell Special Agent Davies about me?"

Her smile betrayed not a hint of slyness, but all he could get from her was a smug, "Nothing but the truth."

At the stark reminder of his duty to give Deke's daughter the full truth, Harry said curtly, "Close the door on your way out, Camille."

Then he reached for the phone one more time, intent on reaching Liane before Agent Davies beat him to the punch.

Chapter 15

Peering from behind the corner of the old bunkhouse, Mac watched Liane walk out with the man he now knew for certain was her lover. Though he hadn't been able to see anything when he'd finally worked up the courage to creep close enough, he'd damned well heard her cries of passion. It disgusted him to know that his wife, still as beautiful as ever, was whoring with some two-bit cowboy, that she would screw the bear-spray-wielding bastard within sight of the house where she lived with the children whose minds she'd poisoned against him.

I'd be well within my rights to kill them both now, to leave their blood-soaked bodies lying in the dirt. Then he could go and take the children. Sooner or later they would come around and realize that everything he'd done had been for them. Eventually, he thought, he could even make them love him. *After all, I'll be the only one they have left.*

But when he noticed the tools that Liane and her lover

were carrying, he pushed aside his fury and focused on what she was saying.

"There's no way we'll find that money, not after the sheriff and his deputies have already searched the place three times."

"If it's anywhere, it has to be in your dad's study," the cowboy insisted. "Maybe hidden in the walls?"

Mac's rage grew white-hot. Not only was the cowboy screwing Liane, he was clearly out to claim the money he'd sacrificed everything for.

She nodded. "I still think you're dead wrong, but Dad did have drywall put in front of the old log walls so he could hang his photos."

He nodded, shifting the tools uncomfortably.

"Let me get that. You're still healing," she said, reaching for the pickax.

"I've got it," he was quick to tell her.

Even from his vantage point, Mac could detect the strain between them.

"Don't be so stubborn," Liane said, taking the pickax from him.

"When they put up the drywall," the cowboy said, "they would've had to build the wall out. Which means there'd be a space behind it."

"If there's a drywall patch, we'll see it," she said. "But don't you think the sheriff and his men would've, too?"

The two of them walked toward the house, still debating, and Mac weighed his options. As badly as he wanted them dead, he had to have that money. Could he take a chance on killing them both and then searching the house by himself? Or would it be better to risk a confrontation now, before they got inside, and force them to do his searching for him?

Armed as he was, he was certain he could control Liane,

but the memory of the tall man jumping him, then nailing him full in the face with the bear spray, had him worried about the potential for another violent surprise.

So take the risk out of the equation, he thought as, heart in throat, he slipped out into the open. *Kill the cowboy right now, while surprise is on your side.*

"Move over, Misty," Liane said as she set down the tools to unlock the back door, "and please stay out from under my feet."

Whining urgently, the dog seemed as tense as she felt, but it was all she could do to handle her own swirling emotions. As furious as she'd been with Jake for believing her father could have found and kept the stolen money, she knew she was not only terrified he was right but angry with herself.

She'd been a fool to sleep with him. No matter how powerful the attraction, how right and inevitable—how incredible—it had felt to make love with him, she knew she could only hurt him by pretending she was capable of getting past what had happened to her and moving forward.

She also knew now that she'd been crazy to think she and Jake could ever maintain a simple friendship. There was no ignoring the way he made her feel and no deluding herself into thinking she could ever push him away without hurting him or that it wouldn't destroy her to see him with another woman.

"You all right?" he asked, clueing her in to the fact that she was standing frozen in place.

"Whatever we find or don't find," he said gently, "I swear to you, I'll be there to help you through it."

Tears came to her eyes as she thought of how much she would miss this caring man and how devastated her kids, who had taken to begging her to "be real nice to Mr. Jake so he can stay with us forever," would be when they were forced to leave him. Her heart shuddered as she thought of giving up the home that had been in her family for more than a century, but she had no hope of affording it on her own, much less growing the business back to the point where it was a going concern. Instead, she would be forced to evict Jake and then leave—perhaps returning to her old job—since she couldn't imagine sticking around this area, living on the fringes of her old life.

The sense of loss and failure, of letting down her father and grandfather, the whole long line of Masons, stole the breath from her lungs. Maybe if she'd taken more of an interest from the start, stayed here to help her dad instead of rushing off straight after college to work for a big corporate hotel—or tried harder to help him out after her return, in spite of his resistance to what he'd called her "fancy new ideas"—he never would've grown desperate enough to...

Grief sideswiped her again, so raw and painful that she found herself saying, "I need a moment. You go in. It's just—it's harder than I thought to come back."

"The first step's always toughest," he said, looking at her with such compassion that she wanted to fall into his arms.

But she didn't allow herself to compound her earlier error. Instead she opened the door, moving aside as Misty nosed her way through. "I'll be right in, I promise. Do you remember the alarm code?"

"I've got it," he told her as he stepped inside to turn off the newly repaired system. "You call if you need me and I'll be back out in a flash."

The smile Liane sent Jake's way didn't touch the sadness in her eyes. As upset as he'd been when she'd compared him to her ex, his anger evaporated at the reminder of the hell she'd been through—and was still going through.

Don't crowd her, he warned himself, *or you could lose her forever.*

A few minutes later, when he looked out to check on her, he found her pacing as she spoke on the phone.

"Whatever you need to say, Sheriff," she was saying, "just go ahead and spit it out."

Assuming that Harry was telling her about the FBI's involvement, he left the door ajar, then went to find a flashlight. Back inside the study, he directed the beam over every inch of drywall, including the areas hidden behind the desk and file cabinet and behind the framed photos. But he found no sign of a recent patch job, nor did he spot anything behind several file boxes in the supply closet.

"Foundation..." he murmured, then looked down, realizing he should have thought of the floor earlier. Though he saw no evidence of loose boards, he realized there was no way he would know for certain whether anything was under there until he took up the big area rug and then pried up every bit of flooring.

It would leave a hell of a mess, he knew, as well as a lot to explain when the FBI came calling. Realizing that his previous plan to move the money if he found it had been a foolish fantasy, he decided he had better discuss things with Liane before he went any further.

As he returned to the back door, he didn't hear her talking, so he stepped outside to look. "Liane?" he called, wondering where she could have gone.

Then he spotted the taillights of her silver Jeep as they disappeared from view.

Chapter 16

As she ended her conversation with Harry, Liane was stopped her in her tracks by the sound of a voice she'd hoped never to hear again. Mac's voice.

"One move, one sound, and you're one dead slut, I swear it."

Shock cascading through her system, she felt something hard pressing into her back. A gun, she thought, a scream on her lips before he grabbed her arm and starting walking her quickly toward her Jeep.

"Try anything and I swear I *will* shoot you," he said. "Now move. We're going for a little ride."

Somehow she managed to stay on her feet, but there was nothing she could do to stop her body's trembling or the nausea threatening to double her over. *It's real this time—no nightmare. Today's the day I die.*

"You want to stay alive?" he asked. "At least a little longer?"

Paralyzed with fear, she couldn't answer.

"I'll take that as a yes," he told her as he opened the driver's door and shoved her behind the wheel.

Shaking her head, she fought to clamp down on her panic. "Just let me go inside and tell him I have to go pick up the kids. That way he won't be suspicious."

Mac's cruel laughter sent her racing heartbeat into overdrive. "You're kidding, right? You take one step toward that house and it's over." His gun still pointed at her, he slipped into the seat behind her. "Take out that phone and call him, tell him you'll be right back. Tell him Cody's sick and you've gone to get him. Tell him whatever you want. Just make it good."

"He'll insist on coming with me," she warned, desperation forcing her voice higher. "No matter what I say."

Mac's slow grin in the rearview was the face of evil. "If you can't manage one simple lie, no problem. I have a score to settle with the bastard anyway. And don't worry, I'll be happy to take his place between your legs."

Liane's vision grayed, her stomach lurching.

"Start driving," he ordered. "Then make your call. And be sure to make your story convincing."

She pulled her keys from her pocket and stabbed them into the ignition. "He'll hear it in my voice that I'm lying."

"He'd better not. Otherwise we *will* go get those kids now, and I swear you'll never see them again."

Alarm streaked through her at the thought that he might mean to harm them. "Please, Mac. Whatever you believe I've done, you've already punished me by—you took my father from me."

"It was his own damned fault. He went for his gun—didn't even give me a chance to ask him about that money he stole. *My* money."

"Whatever he did or didn't do," she said, forcing herself

to keep her focus on saying whatever she had to to save her children, "there's no reason to do this."

"I can think of about two-and-a-half million reasons," he said. "And that's not even counting the most important one—revenge."

As Camille stepped inside Harry's office, she raised her delicate brows. "I've never seen you turn up your nose at Toni's pot roast. Something wrong with it today?"

He looked down at the congealing brown mass, normally his favorite, and shut the take-out container with a snap. "Guess I'm just not hungry."

"You're not getting sick, are you?"

He shook his head, though the burning in his stomach had grown worse than ever. Funny, when he'd convinced himself that talking with Liane would make things better. Maybe if he'd kept on talking, rather than convincing himself he'd already upset her enough for one day...

She gave him a skeptical look. "Your color's kind of off. Maybe you should make an appointment with the doctor."

"If your grandmother's put you up to doing her nagging for her, you can tell her I'm just fine." With no children of his own to "look after him," as his sister put it, she'd come right out and told him it was up to her to see he didn't go to seed. He might have appreciated the thought if Violet's "help" hadn't included sending Hurricane Camille his way.

His grandniece looked worried. "Maybe Grandma's right. You've had a really tough week, and it's only been a few months since Aunt Myrtle—"

"Six months," he said hollowly, feeling every day of the half year since he'd last seen her in the flesh. In dreams he saw her all the time, and even in the daylight he often imagined he glimpsed her thin face with its reassuring smile.

"Why don't you go home and lie down for a little while?" she suggested. "I can give you a call when Special Agent Davies gets here."

"I imagine you'd like that," he groused. "Give you another chance to chat with your new friend about me."

She smiled. "Come on, Uncle Harry. I was only teasing about that. I swear I didn't tell her anything except how you're a real sweetheart, underneath that grouchy exterior."

"The hell I am. Now, did you come in here for any reason in particular? Aside from irritating me, that is?"

Still smiling, she nodded and passed him a message. "Sure. I thought you might get a kick out of this one. Lady called in with an *urgent* problem."

"What kind of problem?"

Camille rolled her eyes. "She says that when she and her husband came home a little bit ago her coffee pot was empty. And, even worse, apparently she'd had her heart set on a honey-glazed donut, but somebody'd swiped the last one from the box."

She laughed, as she usually did at the more absurd calls. But if she'd hoped he would join in, she was disappointed.

"You're seriously bothering me about that? Now? Don't you have some filing out there or something?"

She sighed and left him, hurrying her steps when the phone on her desk started ringing.

Before Harry could get up the gumption to toss his lunch in the trash, Camille called, "Line two for you. Bob Carpenter, and he sounds really mad."

Wondering what was bothering the normally easygoing retiree—who had occasionally joined him and Deke for breakfast—Harry picked up. "Wallace here. What can I do for you, Bob?"

"You can get a man out here, and I don't mean tomorrow."

Taken aback at his friend's tone, Harry glanced down at the name on the message Camille had handed to him. "This isn't about Becky's missing donut, is it?"

"Hell, no, it isn't about my wife's stupid donuts. But she wouldn't quit squawking, so I checked things out and found a busted window latch in the back. So I checked, and a pistol's missing from my gun case."

That was when it hit Harry, like a hard pop to the sternum. This was definitely no laughing matter. Because the Carpenters lived out on Black Oak Road, all too close to the Masons.

Heart pounding, he murmured a promise that he would send a man out ASAP and quickly hung up, thirty-eight years of law enforcement instincts screaming that the theft was no coincidence. McCleary was alive and had come back with a vengeance, either out of desperation to find his missing money or to finally finish what he'd started when he'd first tried to kill Liane.

Jake was just pulling his phone from his pocket when it started ringing and Liane's name popped up on the screen.

"What's wrong?" he asked, ignoring Misty's attempt to push her head beneath his free hand. "I saw you drive off. What the hell—where are you going?"

"He was my father. I can't do this." Her words clinked together, like ice cubes against glass. "And I don't want you in there, digging through my house."

The phone beeped to signal that he had another call. Ignoring it, he stepped outside, the blood rushing in his ears and the big dog right beside him. "Come back, Liane, please. You're upset. Let's talk this through, and then if you still don't want to—"

"It's not that—it's Cody. The school nurse called to say he's sick. I have to go and get him. I have to go right now."

"Come on back and let me take you. You shouldn't be driving when you're upset."

"No!" she said, far too sharply.

"Liane, think of your kids. If you're in a wreck, who will they have to—"

"You," she said emphatically. "They'll have *you,* Jake. That's what I want. Remember."

A white-hot current of alarm burned through him. "What are you saying, Liane?"

With a beep in his ear, the call disconnected. Ignoring the ringing of the landline inside, he tried frantically to call her back. When his calls kept rolling to her voice mail, he reached for his keys and raced for his pickup. His heart was hammering a warning that if he didn't get to her quickly, he would regret it forever.

"Out of the truck, Misty," he shouted when the dog jumped into the pickup bed, her tail wagging with excitement. As she reluctantly obeyed, the phone in his hand started ringing. "Liane," he said, slipping behind the wheel. "Thank God. What's—"

"Jake—it's Harry here." The sheriff shouted to make himself heard over a siren's wail. "I've been trying to reach you to let you know—"

"I have to catch Liane." The pickup's engine roared to life. "She just took off in her Jeep. Then she called and told me—"

"You don't understand. It's—"

Jake talked over him. *"No, you* don't understand. Something's *wrong.* I have to catch her before she—"

"Shut up and listen to me, Whittaker!" Harry boomed. "It's McCleary. I think he's alive and on his way there."

"McCleary?" Panic speared him. Could Liane's ex have grabbed her? "I thought he was long gone. Or dead."

"That's why I'm calling. I'm on my way out to the ranch

now. We've had a report of a break-in next door, and Bob Carpenter says he has a gun missing. School's been contacted to keep the children inside and in sight, and not to release them until a deputy gets there, but I couldn't get hold of Liane."

"He has her. That has to be it." Nothing else accounted for her abrupt change in behavior. His blood running cold, Jake threw the truck back into Park and bailed out. He was going to need a weapon of his own. "She said she was going to the school to pick up Cody. That might've been a lie, but either way I'm going after them before they get too far."

"You stay put," Harry ordered. "I'm en route, and I've got deputies dispatched, too."

"I'll be damned if I'll let him hurt her," Jake swore.

"You're in way over your head on this, Jake. You'll get her killed. Maybe yourself, too."

"If I don't move right now, she's as good as dead already." His life would be over, too, if he couldn't save her.

"You have to let me do this. This is my responsibility, all of it."

Before Jake could ask what he meant, Harry added, "I'm only ten, maybe fifteen, minutes out at most. It's possible that I can intercept them. If not, I'll pick you up and we can go from there."

"That's ten or fifteen minutes for Mac to take her God knows where." Jake couldn't stand to think about what he would do to Liane then or how terrified she must be. How could he have taken his eyes off her even for a moment?

"I'm—I'm ordering—" Gasping for breath, the sheriff struggled to get the words out. "Ordering—you—Jake. Stay—"

A pained grunt was followed by a thump as if he'd dropped the phone.

"What's wrong, Harry? Harry?" Jake shouted, but no matter how he strained his ears, he heard only the keening of the siren. *Not this. Not now,* he thought, recalling how exhausted the man had looked of late, how worn by the burden of his best friend's murder.

"Pull over!" he yelled. "Pull off the road now, Harry. I'm calling 9-1-1." When there was no response, he added, "Can you hear me?"

As the siren continued to wail, Jake thought he made out another low moan. A moment later there was a banging sound and the line went dead. Had Harry fumbled the phone and disconnected—or crashed into the trees that lined the lightly traveled road?

Though finding Liane was his priority, Jake called 9-1-1 and reported what he'd heard, along with his best estimate of the sheriff's location. By the time he was finished making certain the dispatcher understood Liane's situation, too, he'd collected the borrowed handgun from the cabin and was speeding down Black Oak Road in the direction she had turned.

As he drove he lowered the windows, thinking he might hear something his eyes missed, and racked his brain trying to imagine where McCleary might have taken her. Did he really mean to snatch the children, as Liane's call had suggested? Thankful that Harry had moved quickly to see to their safety, Jake considered the possibility that McCleary believed Liane knew the location of the money. Or maybe it had never been about the money. Maybe she'd been right to think it was the desire for vengeance that drove him.

Jake tasted bile at the thought that McCleary might simply shoot her and dump the body somewhere, just as he had left Deke. Even more nightmarish was the possibility that he would take her someplace where he could pay her back for her imagined sins with hours of brutal torture, while Jake searched frantically, as helpless to save her as he'd been to rescue his men.

He slowed as he approached a crossroads, looking for any clue that a vehicle might have recently turned off, heading either toward the river or the Smuggler's Gulch Trailhead. Spotting no traffic or even a hint of telltale dust above the smaller dirt roads, he made the difficult decision to remain on Black Oak, heading toward town—and the school.

Spotting a blue-gray blur in his rearview mirror, he saw that Misty must have jumped back into the pickup bed when he'd gone inside to grab the gun. Nothing he could do about that now. He just kept driving, panic clawing its way along his backbone. What if he'd been wrong to go straight? What if Mac had forced Liane to pull off into one of the narrow driveways leading toward someone's vacation cabin or a hidden hiking trail? And there were other turn-offs ahead, other choices that could as easily prove wrong.

Images of Liane suffering at that bastard's hands hammering at his temples, Jake pictured himself blowing McCleary's brains out or, better yet, pounding his face to pulp. But as violent as his rage was, he quickly realized that right now, raw emotion was the enemy. He had to push aside his feelings and think clearly or he really would lose her forever....

And two beautiful kids would lose the only parent they knew, just as he'd lost his own mother so many years before.

Liane's voice whispered in his memory, saying that the kids would have *him. That's what I want. Remember.*

"They'll have both of us," he promised, voice breaking. "Because I swear I'm going to bring you home alive."

* * *

"Are you deliberately trying to piss me off?" Mac accused Liane. "I heard what you said, telling him my kids—my son—will have *him?* What the hell were you thinking?"

"I don't know. I guess I *wasn't* thinking," she said as she continued driving, hating herself for backsliding into the same useless excuses she had once used to placate him. She'd faced down a forest fire, killed a desperate ex-con before he could kill *her,* but in the face of Mac's threats she was as helpless as she'd been the night he'd left her to die.

"Don't lie to me. You *were* thinking," he said. "Thinking of one more way to screw me over. Now give me that damned phone so I can call him back."

"What? You're going to—"

"Now that we've put a little distance between him and us, it's time to give him a chance to buy your freedom. So do you trust your lover, Liane? Do you trust that two-bit wrangler with your life?"

"I don't understand."

"You wouldn't," he said with a grunt of disgust. "I want the money your father stole from me, every last dime of it. And your cowboy's going to bring it to me—if he ever wants to see you again."

"And then you'll let us go?"

Rather than answering, he asked, "What do you think, Liane? Will he bring the money, or will he sell you out?"

"He'll come," she said hollowly, realizing that her attempt to warn him with her phone call had been doomed from the start. Even after she had made the choice to leave him, to marry another man and bear his children, Jake had never given up on her. And now, regardless of the cost, he would keep fighting long after she surrendered. *Because that's what real love does.*

The thought of his strength, his selflessness and his passion to protect drove the weakness from her body. If Jake saw something in her worth risking—even sacrificing—his own life for, how could she sit there like a trembling, passive victim and let him walk straight into a situation that would surely get him killed?

"There's no need to involve him," she said. "We don't need him to get the money."

"Don't lie to me to try to save him."

"I'm not—"

"I *heard* you. The money's in your father's study."

"That was Jake's theory," she argued. "But I'm telling you, he's wrong."

"Make a right here," he ordered, pointing toward a rutted gravel track so overgrown that she had already zipped past before she spotted it.

Cursing her, Mac ordered, "Turn around right now, or I swear, this will go far worse than you ever imagined."

Realizing that nothing she could say was going to make him listen, she sucked in a deep breath and mashed down the accelerator, her pulse jumping along with the accelerator needle.

"What the hell do you think you're doing?" he roared.

"You think I'm going to let you lure Jake to some dark, deserted spot and kill us both the moment he shows up?" she asked, her voice shaking with the effort of defying her worst nightmare. "You want to shoot me? Fine. Do it now and let's end this together—if you're willing to leave our kids without either of their parents."

If he pulled the trigger, at least her death would count for something. Jake and her children would be safe from Mac's insanity.

In an instant he grabbed her hair and brutally yanked her skull back against the headrest. Screaming at the sudden pain, she reflexively jerked the wheel and stamped on the brakes.

Tires squealing, they shot across the line into the other lane. At the same moment an oncoming RV emerged from around the upcoming bend. As Mac let go of her, a horn blared—far too close—and she saw the driver and his passenger's rounded mouths and terrified eyes.

Instinct kicked in—she couldn't cost an innocent couple their lives—and before she realized she was even steering clear, the brown-and-white RV was sliding past them. In her rearview she saw it straighten and disappear farther down the road.

Heart jackhammering against her rib cage, she was shaking so hard, she had no choice except to pull onto the shoulder.

The moment she came to a stop, Mac screamed at her, "You crazy bitch!"

Hearing the threat in his voice, she turned to look and saw his right fist flying toward her just in time for her to flinch away. More enraged than ever for having missed her, Mac leaned between the seats, shoving the gun up beneath her jaw.

"I'm not *asking* you a damned thing. I'm telling you. Turn the car around now and pull off the road where I said, or I swear to you, when your cowboy shows up, all he'll get for his efforts is the shock of finding your brains spattered everywhere—before I kill him."

Even worse than the threat of her own death was the idea of how devastated Jake would be to find her, and how destroyed her children would be by yet another brutal loss. Maybe she'd been wrong before, too quick to give up hope. Every minute she remained alive was another minute she might find some way to escape, or at least to convince him to leave the children and Jake out of this.

"Move!" Mac bellowed at her.

She forced herself to nod, the movement painful with the pistol's muzzle grinding into her jawbone. When he pulled it back, she managed to say, "Just give me—let me breathe a minute."

"You don't have ten seconds," he said. "Not if you don't listen."

Casting up a silent prayer, she checked for traffic and then made a U-turn. In moments she turned, and thick evergreen branches scraped along the Jeep's sides as it wallowed downhill on the overgrown and deeply rutted trail.

"Over there, behind that boulder," he said, pointing out a patch of shadow, where no one would ever see or hear them. Where he could leave her for the animals, just as he had left her father's blood-soaked corpse.

Chills raced through her body as the memory flashed before her eyes.

"Go on, pull in," he urged. "Then give me the keys and we'll make that call."

We, he'd said, which meant he didn't plan to kill her. *At least not until he uses me as bait.*

Would there be a chance for her to speak on the phone, an opportunity to warn Jake that regardless of anything Mac promised, he planned to kill them both? She glanced up, meeting his gaze in the rearview mirror. In the cruel depths of his eyes she saw nothing but her death—hers and Jake's both—and for all she knew, he would make good on his threat and go after the kids, too.

Once she'd pulled in and shut off the engine, he pointed the gun between the seat backs and held out his other hand. "The keys," he reminded her. "Now."

"I'm telling you," she said. "Jake was wrong. The money's never been at the house. It was in the—"

"You're lying!"

When he drew back his arm to hit her, she reacted too fast for thought, flinging the keys as hard as she could, straight into his face. With an enraged shout, he deflected them, but the split second's distraction was all she needed to jump out of the car and take off running.

She knew it was insanity. He was far bigger, far stronger—and armed. Thinking it would be harder to hit a zig-zagging target, she raced around the boulder and threaded her way through tightly packed trees back toward the road, praying that her smaller size and greater agility would give her an advantage. If she could only survive these first few moments, she could lose herself, hide herself, and then flag down a motorist when she heard one coming.

But the thudding footsteps just behind her assured her she would never get the chance.

Chapter 17

Slumped over in the front seat of his cruiser, Harry weakly pushed the deflated airbag away from his face. With the movement, pain poleaxed him, an explosion in his sternum that had him clutching at his chest.

Too much pain, he thought miserably, regretting not the things he'd done but only their unintended costs—costs that might now include the life of his best friend's daughter.

Sitting in the seat beside him, Myrtle stroked his sweat-dampened hair with her spectral hand and offered him her saddest smile, a smile that told him that for all his attempts to shield her from his burdens, she understood his struggle.

But in those beautiful brown eyes he'd loved so long, he read a final request. *You have to stay strong, Harry... strong enough to do what's right.*

"I will, I swear it," he said through gritted teeth, funneling every atom of stubbornness into reaching for the radio.

Fresh agony eclipsed his vision, and stars roared to

the surface of the sudden darkness. An instant later they were spiraling together, forming a ball of blinding brilliance. With his eyes scrunched closed against the white light, it came to him that Myrtle wasn't the only one urging him to fight.

In an echo of his nightmares, Deke Mason once again reached out his hand. Reached and then pointed straight at Harry—a terrible reminder of his guilt.

Sunlight gleamed off metal, and Jake's stomach dropped when he spotted the car nose-down in a shallow culvert not far off the road. The lights were still flashing, though the siren had fallen silent, and there wasn't a single other vehicle in sight.

The choice tore at him. Uncertain he was even driving in the right direction, did he delay his search for Liane, giving Mac an even greater lead? Or did he drive past a man he might be able to save, quite possibly leaving him to die?

Call in the location and keep going, instinct urged him, but at the last moment he pulled over, unable to drive past without seeing if Harry needed help.

Jake jumped down from his truck and firmly ordered Misty, "Stay."

As he hurried toward the car, he shouted, "Harry? It's Jake Whittaker. Are you in there?"

Hearing no answer and spotting no sign of movement, he scrambled down the low embankment, noting the slightly crumpled hood and the white steam that indicated a punctured radiator. Despite the damage, the wreck appeared survivable.

"Anyone there?" he called, pulling out his cell phone and dialing 9-1-1 again. Wading through weeds, he approached the front door as he gave the dispatcher his location.

"I have an ambulance and deputies en route—you should be hearing them any minute," she said, clearly struggling to maintain her professional composure. "Is Sheriff Wallace all right? Is he alive?"

"Appears unconscious," he said as he approached the window and spotted the deflated mass of an airbag and then Harry, slumped on his right side. Chalky pale and beaded with sweat, he had the slack expression of a man who was out cold—or dead. "Let me see what I can do and I'll call you right back." Pocketing the phone to free his hands, Jake struggled to open the driver's door. When it stuck stubbornly, he made his way to the other side, praying he had reached the sheriff in time—and praying even harder that this delay wouldn't cost Liane her life.

To his immense relief, the passenger door opened. Leaning inside, he reached carefully and laid his fingers against Harry's throat. He felt a pulse, thank God, though it was thready and erratic.

"Harry, it's Jake. Can you hear me?" he asked as he scanned the man for injuries. Seeing no blood or any obvious fractures, he tried shaking Harry's shoulder, though he didn't expect a response.

To his surprise, the sheriff grabbed his hand, his gray eyes shooting open. "You need to go see Myrtle," he said weakly. "She'll tell you where I... She's a good woman, Jake. The best. But she never did like camping. Hardly used that fifth wheel parked out in the garage..."

Alarmed by Harry's confusion, Jake hastened to assure him, "I know you loved her, Harry. Everyone knows how much—"

Grimacing, the sheriff shook his head. "When you see her, you tell her I'm sorry. I never meant to hurt any—anyone else. I only wanted more time...." His words faded into gibberish, his eyes growing unfocused.

"Everything's going to be fine," Jake said, relieved beyond measure to hear the first faint strains of a siren.

"No." Harry fought to raise his head. "Not for Liane. Not unless you find... You've gotta give it back. You've got to find it—for her."

Jake tensed, wondering if there could be more to Harry's ramblings than the delusions of a dying man. "Find what?"

"Investors never would've seen a dime anyway. Not after the lawyers..."

"The money," Jake said, thinking of how haggard Harry had looked, how often he had spoken of his own responsibility in the wake of his friend's death. Could there be something more going on than guilt over a misplaced fax and his failure to take Liane's first phone call seriously? "You know exactly where Deke hid it, don't you?"

As the siren drew nearer, the sheriff moaned and closed his eyes, pressing the heel of his hand against his chest.

"Please, Harry. For Liane's sake. If Deke hid it in his study, tell me. That money might end up being the only thing that can save her life."

"Not Deke. Never Deke," Harry choked out. "He... turned it in...gave every dime to me."

Pure adrenaline shooting through her system, Liane made it farther than she expected.

Ducking around another tree trunk, she shoved through some low branches. But with the flutter of leaves obscuring her sight, she missed her footing, stumbling over loose rock and gasping as she crashed to her knees.

Mac was on her in an instant, tackling her from behind and knocking her to the stony ground. She struggled to get away, but he struck again and again, a frenzied rain of blows that had her pleading and struggling. "Stop! Please!"

But by now he was beyond listening. When he grabbed her hair and yanked it, instinct made her fight him, her nails scoring bloody gouges just beneath his eyes.

"Bitch!" he shouted, and before she understood what was happening, his red face was in hers and his hands were squeezing her throat. Squeezing so hard she couldn't scream, couldn't fill her lungs, as he shook her like a terrier with a rodent in its jaws.

She fought to draw breath, to dig her nails into his hands—anything to loosen his grip. With her empty lungs screaming for oxygen, the trees grayed out before her and bright spangles of color burst across her vision.

"Why do you always have to push me?" he screamed, his voice distorted by the rushing river of her pain and panic. "Push, push, push, until you leave me no choice!"

As the gray haze turned to black and the roaring in her head grew louder, Liane wanted to scream that he had always, from the first, had choices. Choices he had used to steal, to strike, to blame everyone but himself. Choices he had used to kill her father, and to take her from her children and the man she'd loved forever, even if she hadn't realized that until just now.

And in that moment, all the fear, the shame and self-blame she had lived with for so long crumbled. With her body failing, her heart reached for a memory of Jake and her children's faces....

And her hand stretched out, until her fingers bumped something hard and wrapped around it.

Chapter 18

"Where?" Jake demanded, shaking the sheriff to rouse him. "Where did you hide it, Harry?"

"My wife—it was for—the first transplant failed. The kidney died, and the dialysis was—it was killing her. But the insurance said we'd…maxed out, and she was so far down the list…I couldn't let her go. She's everything… all I had."

"You took the money to save your wife," Jake said flatly, though he wondered, if the woman he loved were dying, could he have resisted the temptation?

"We got her into a program—Asian—they promised they could get a living donor if we…if we flew over there."

"You told everyone you were going for an experimental drug protocol, but it was really for a black-market kidney," Jake said, sickened by the memory of a photo he had once seen of poor villagers lined up showing off their scars. According to the news report, some had netted as little as a few hundred dollars, while the facilities that bro-kered the transplants charged tens of thousands—some-times hundreds of thousands—for their services. "Deke knew, didn't he?"

"Not at first, but he…he figured out I hadn't turned in the money. Tried to give him what was left, but he re-fused…."

"So you're the one who's been paying off his bills in cash."

"The rest—Liane and the kids should have it…."

"So where is it, Harry? Tell me, damn it," Jake asked as the ambulance came into view. "McCleary could be kill-ing her right now!"

Eyelids shuttering once more, the sheriff's lips moved. Bending low to hear him, Jake barely made out the words, but when he tried to rouse Harry to get him to repeat them, there was no response.

Seconds later the EMTs were rushing past him. Still reeling from the sheriff's confession, Jake stopped the driver of the ambulance and asked if he had spotted Li-ane's silver Jeep on his way.

The man shook his balding head. "I don't think so, no. Now step out of the way. This patient needs—"

"You're *sure* you didn't see that Jeep?" Jake pressed, still not budging. "A woman's life might depend on your memory. That's who Sheriff Wallace came out here to help."

"Pretty sure, yeah. Now, I really have to go."

"Thanks." Stepping out of the man's path, Jake rushed back to his pickup. Still standing in the bed, Misty wagged her tail in greeting. "Up in the front," Jake told her, not wanting to worry about her falling out if it came down to a chase.

But before he could chase Mac and Liane, he would have to find them.

As the dog hopped up into the passenger seat, Jake wondered if the driver might have been mistaken, but his gut was telling him that he'd been wrong from the beginning. McCleary hadn't risked coming back for Liane because he'd suddenly developed paternal feelings.

He had returned for either revenge or the money. If it was Liane's life he wanted, Jake reluctantly admitted there was no way to guess where he would take her or whether he'd killed her already. But if he wanted to find the missing millions, why would he leave with Liane in the first place?

Unless he'd planned to return to the homestead as soon as Jake was gone?

Could that be right? Could Liane's phone call really have been meant to lure him from the house? Jake pictured McCleary pulling off the road somewhere, then watching from some hidden spot until Jake's truck vanished from view. In that case, he was probably back at the ranch right now, demanding that Liane produce the stolen money.

"And when she can't…" he said aloud, his mouth drying as he thought of Harry, pretending he knew nothing, while all along he'd had the answers. With a squeal of tires, Jake turned the truck around and sped back toward the homestead. He couldn't afford to waste his focus on questions of guilt or blame.

All he could do was pray that he was right—and that he wasn't already too late.

When stone met skull, the impact reverberated, running the length of Liane's arm. The pressure on her throat vanished as Mac fell to his side with a grunt, blood staining the jagged rock she was still clutching for dear life.

Crawling away from him, she sucked in greedy gulps

of air, her vision clearing and her strength returning with the oxygen. But Mac was already rousing, moaning curses and struggling to push himself onto his hands and knees.

She raised the rock again, her arms shaking so hard she could barely lift it. Getting up onto her knees, she felt the adrenaline surging through her body and the muscles coiling, giving her the chance to save herself, to keep her children and Jake safe from Mac forever....

She could slam the sharp-edged rock against his head again and again, until bone yielded and brain splattered. It was no more than he deserved, a brutal payback for the fists that had battered her flesh, for the bullet that had stolen her chance for future children, for the murder that had taken her father away forever.

When he turned to look at her, bright streamers of blood pouring down his face, she hesitated, revolted to her core to think that he'd reduced her to such savagery—made her a stranger to herself. And in that single moment the pain and confusion in his face morphed into fury, and he lunged for her, grabbing for her arm and sending the rock tumbling.

She jerked away, springing to her feet and running, racing toward the road. Behind her, she heard him bellowing, "It was all for you! All for my family! Why can't you understand that?"

Despite their heat, his words were slurred, and—when she dared to look back—she saw him staggering and crashing through thick branches that slowed his clumsy progress. It was only then that she began to think she might make it, might reach the road and find help....

And then the woods exploded, the trees and rocks around her echoing with gunfire.

Intent on the road ahead, Jake scarcely noticed when Misty jumped up onto the seat and started whining, thrusting her muzzle out the open window.

When she yelped, he said, "Be quiet," and snapped a sharp look her way.

The dog was craning her head to look intently at a break in the trees they'd just driven past. She barked again, the high-pitched sound reminding him of the last time he had seen her react that way—only hours earlier, when Liane had stood just outside his cabin door.

"Liane!" he shouted, and at the sound of her mistress's name, Misty put her front paws on the door frame, gathering herself for what could easily be a fatal leap out of the speeding truck.

"No," he ordered sharply, braking hard as he pulled onto the shoulder.

Gravel still crunching beneath the tires, he made a grab for the dog, but his healing right arm wasn't strong enough, and she scrabbled out the window and raced toward the woods.

Jake craned his head, scanning the brush and trees ahead but spotting nothing. Could he have been wrong about the dog reacting to Liane's presence? Was it possible Misty was chasing some animal instead? Unwilling to take the chance, he grabbed his gun and ran after her, desperate not to lose her.

He'd only made it a few steps when he saw bushes near the tree line sway. An instant later a slim figure burst from cover, stopping short as she spotted first the dog and then him.

"Jake!" Liane screamed, her hair as wild as her eyes. Her face was swollen, desperate and tear-streaked. "Get down! He's right behind me!"

Despite her warning, Jake charged toward her, unable to think of anything but getting her to safety.

Misty rushed past Liane, then slid to a stiff-legged stop, her hackles rising and a deep growl rumbling in her chest.

Liane staggered to a stop, a look of shock and confusion washing the color from her face. "Jake," she cried, rubbing at a spot behind her back. "I think I'm—"

"I'll kill you, bitch!" Mac shouted, bursting from the trees behind her.

The moment he showed his blood-streaked face, Misty charged him—a barking, snapping distraction that had him turning his gun on her.

Before Mac could shoot the dog, Jake lunged past Liane and fired on McCleary. When his first shots missed, Mac crouched and took aim—setting his sights not on Jake but on Liane.

But he never got a chance to fire, because Jake's next shot caught him, not in the chest, where he'd been aiming, but just beneath the eye. Jerking backward, Mac dropped his weapon and sat down hard. His body teetered back and forth, the rage on his face giving way to a blank stare.

Still holding the gun on him, Jake raised his voice to make himself heard over the dog's barking, "Hands up and we'll get you help."

But Mac didn't seem to hear. Instead, he toppled onto his side, where he convulsed weakly and went still.

Jake rushed in, grabbing the man's fallen weapon and then checking for a pulse. Shaking his head, he said to Liane, "He's gone."

She stared, wide-eyed, the color draining from her battered face. "It—it's really over?"

Turning away from the dead man, Jake rushed to Liane and gathered her in his arms. "It's all over," he promised. "He'll never hurt you again."

Their gazes locked as she cried out, and he felt the warm stickiness on his palm. Blood, all over her back.

"Liane, what happened?" But before the question was out, her legs folded beneath her and her head tipped back, exposing her bruised throat as she turned to dead weight in his arms.

She couldn't be dead, too. A bolt of blue-hot panic blasted through him. After all they'd been through and everything she'd suffered, she couldn't possibly be gone, too, especially not now, when they'd come so close to finally getting things right between them.

"Wake up," he pleaded, lowering her to the ground and checking for a pulse. Finding nothing, he cursed, wanting to revive McCleary just to kill him again, to make him suffer. But he couldn't give up on Liane—he refused to, so he checked again, praying for all he was worth....

This time he felt it. A bumping, faint and rapid, but her heart was beating. After making sure she was breathing, too, he rolled her onto her side to check the damage to her back.

Blood was oozing from an entry wound near the base of her rib cage, on the right side. No exit wound that he could see, but he quickly stripped off his shirt, balling it up and applying pressure to stanch the flow.

"Stay back," he ordered Misty, as the dog tried to nose her way in, whining and licking Liane's forehead.

As the dog backed off, he pulled out his phone to call for help. But both his training and his instincts told him that by the time another ambulance made it here, it would be too late.

As he struggled to lift her, he glared at McCleary's body. "I'll send the authorities for you later, but I hope like hell the buzzards find you first."

Chapter 19

As Liane drifted, she heard her father demanding that she wake up and get moving or she would miss the school bus, heard her mother urging, "Hurry, or we won't have time for waffles."

Later there were others, strangers speaking of transfusions and surgery, then familiar voices encouraging her to open her eyes. But fatigue weighed down her lids, and she couldn't make her mouth work, couldn't pluck more than a few words from the torrent that washed past her.

It was far easier to ride the ebb and flow of pain, to sink down into the black comfort of oblivion. In this refuge time meant nothing, so she had no idea how long it had been until she became aware once more of people talking somewhere nearby. Tethered as loosely as a balloon to consciousness, she wasn't certain who they were. She only knew she loved them more than anything on earth.

"Why won't she wake up?" the first asked, high and piping. "Why won't she look at the pictures we made her?"

"She's working hard on getting better. We just have to keep doing our part, saying prayers and hoping."

"That's what you said last time. Cody says..."

"What does Cody say? Come on, now. You can tell me, Giggle Girl."

Jake, thought Liane, *it's Jake, talking to Kenzie....*

"He says Mommy's going to heaven, just like Grandpa. He says she's going to ride Buttercup and see the carrots growing upside-down and the peppermint mountains and all the other cool stuff."

"We don't know that, Kenzie. The doctors said your mom could wake up any—"

"I don't want her to leave without me," Kenzie sobbed. "I want to go with her—and Grandpa, too."

"Then who would keep me company? And your brother? How could we all be a family, like your mommy wanted, without you?"

"Then she has to stay here with us! You and her can get married, and we can all be a real family with a mom and a dad and everything!"

"It's what I want, too, Kenzie," he said gently, "more than anything, but sometimes, what we want can't come true, no matter how hard we..."

As the sound of her daughter's weeping overrode his words, Liane's body shuddered, sending a blast of competing sensations ricocheting through her: the crisp cotton of the sheets, the dryness of her lips, the tight itch of a sore spot on her back. But it was the emotion pouring into her that had her fighting to open her eyes, to reach out and—

"Her hand moved! She's awake!" Kenzie cried.

"Sometimes," Jake warned, "it's like when you kick the covers when you're sleeping."

From somewhere deep inside her words formed like tiny bubbles, forcing their way through what felt like thick mud before rising to the surface. "And sometimes," she managed, her voice a threadbare whisper as her eyes took in their hazy figures, "sometimes it means you've fought your way back to everything you love."

Though the nurses scolded them repeatedly about "tiring the patient," there was little Jake could do to dampen Kenzie's joyful squeals, along with Em's and Cody's when they returned from their brief foray to the hospital cafeteria. There were tears and hugs, joy and relief, until finally Liane's strength subsided and she fell into a blessedly natural slumber.

As she regained her strength over the next few days, Jake came as often as he could, sometimes bringing the children and at other times returning on his own. Aware that the time wasn't right to talk about everything that had happened, much less what might happen next between them, he contented himself with talking about the ordinary details of life and helping her do the things she still found difficult, such as walking the hallway with her IV stand, and—once he judged her stamina sufficient—giving in to her pleas to help wash her long hair.

After they were finished she sat up in a padded chair, resting while he carefully worked a wide-toothed comb through the sweetly scented, damp brown waves. Finally she sighed.

"Feel better?" he asked.

Nodding, she reached out to catch his hand, her blue eyes filling with tears. "You've been so good to me, and so wonderful with the kids," she said, "but this isn't right, I can't—can't keep letting you do all this when I can't—there's no way we can ever—"

He squeezed her hand. "There are things we need to talk

about. Things I've been waiting until you're well enough to tell you."

She sighed, then nodded, looking apprehensive.

He began with the hardest news. "Harry Wallace passed away. They say it was his heart."

"Harry? Oh, no. That's terrible."

"There's worse," he said, before explaining, as gently as he knew how, about Harry's misappropriation of the money her father had turned in.

"Then, my father—" Fresh grief leached her returning color. "He tried to do the right thing."

"He did. And the bulk of the money was found where Harry hid it, underneath the flooring of an old camper he had stored in his garage."

She closed her eyes. "I know he loved his wife, but if he hadn't—if Mac had known the money was out of his reach, he never would've come here. Never would've killed my father, and—"

Jake gathered her into his arms, stroking her damp hair until her trembling subsided. "I'm so sorry, Liane. I know this is hard. Maybe we should talk about it later."

"No," she said, pulling away from him, visibly steeling herself for what she had to say. "I need you to understand, I'm going to have to leave again, to sell the ranch to pay back the money Harry put down on the taxes and—and I'm going back to my old job in Las Vegas."

He saw in her face what that would cost her, and he swore to himself that he wouldn't let it happen. "There was a pretty substantial reward for capturing your ex and his buddies," he told her, "and when I led the FBI to the money, it turns out there was a reward for that, too. The agent put my name in for it. But, Liane, that money's yours, to cover what Harry paid on those bills so you can stay here. To save the ranch for your kids."

"But I can't—there's no way. The business has been slipping away for so long, and besides that, I could never hope to run it on my own the way my dad did."

"Not alone," he admitted. "But what if you had help? What if you could do things better?"

"After everything you've done already, you're offering to give up your own career?" she asked in amazement.

He laughed and took her hands in his. "Liane, I *hate* my work. I'm bored stiff. I want to be outdoors again, out in the forest. And leading tourists on horseback tours, sharing everything I know about these mountains, sounds almost perfect."

She smiled at him, her color returning. "Almost?"

"For it to work, I'd need your help full-time—your ideas and your expertise to make Equine Adventures bigger and better than it ever was. We can remodel the old cabins into first-class accommodations the way you were always trying to convince your dad to do, and add a gourmet chuck wagon to do high-end sunset dinners for the well-heeled types from the lodge."

"You've been plotting with Em, haven't you?"

He nodded. "While you were unconscious, I had a lot of time to plan."

"To daydream, you mean," she said with a shake of her head. "But what you're suggesting—it's risky. And it would take a lot of money."

"Em wants to invest, to buy a minority share, and then she'll start referring clients from the lodge and adding package deals once we get things going. And I have some savings, too, to throw in. Since my grandmother's property in Tahoe finally sold, I've been looking for a good place to—"

"I can't take your money, Jake. I can't—"

He smiled and went to his knees, gazing up into the

beautiful face he'd been terrified would be taken from him forever. "Don't you understand? Whatever's mine is yours, Liane. My heart, my soul, everything I have to offer. Because I want to marry you. I want to be your husband, if you'll have me. I'll work at your side—or, hell, if you really want to give up the ranch and take another job anywhere, I'll go with you and keep translating."

"If I thought there was any way to do it," she said, emotion shimmering in her gaze, "I'd keep my family's legacy forever. And I love you so much, Jake, I do, but I—"

"Then say yes. Say yes and be my wife."

When she shook her head, his heart plunged toward jagged bedrock, threatening to shatter. Could she really be rejecting him again?

"I can't," she said, tears streaming, "because of what Mac—the scars you saw—I can never give you children. Children of your own."

"I figured that much out already, but don't you understand? It doesn't matter to me. Only *you* do."

"But you'd be—you're meant to be a father. It's what you've always dreamed of."

"Then, damn it, let me be a father to your children. Let me give them my name and be the dad they've never had. And let me be the man you've always deserved, the one you should have—"

"But, Jake, I—" She shook her head. "Are you really *sure* about this?"

"Are you *kidding?*" Rising to his feet, he told her, "For five long days I prayed and hoped and hugged those children whenever Em brought them to visit. When she took them home, I stayed here. I spent every minute of every night just watching you breathe, praying that I'd—that we'd get one more chance to finally get this thing right. Well, now we have it, Liane, so tell me, after everything we've been through, are you really going to let that bastard win?"

Shaking her head, she somehow got to her still-unsteady feet and then stepped into his arms.

"Not on your life," she whispered, standing on tiptoe to claim a kiss so sweet, so right, so perfect, that the memories gave way, allowing the shared dream of their future the space it needed to unfurl.

* * * * *

COMING NEXT MONTH
from Harlequin® Romantic Suspense
AVAILABLE NOVEMBER 13, 2012

#1731 CHRISTMAS CONFIDENTIAL
Holiday Protector by Marilyn Pappano
A Chance Reunion by Linda Conrad
Two stories of private investigators hot on the trails of the women they love...just in time for Christmas!

#1732 COLTON SHOWDOWN
The Coltons of Eden Falls
Marie Ferrarella
Tate Colton expected to take down the bad guys when he went undercover. But he never expected to fall for the woman he came to rescue.

#1733 O'HALLORAN'S LADY
Fiona Brand
When evidence comes to light that Jenna's stalker is also linked with the death of ex-detective Marc's wife and child, he suddenly has a very personal reason to stay close.

#1734 NO ESCAPE
Meredith Fletcher
To track down a serial killer, homicide detective Heath Boxer teams up with the latest victim's sister... and finds more than just a partner.

You can find more information on upcoming Harlequin® titles, free excerpts and more at www.Harlequin.com.

HRSCNM1112

REQUEST YOUR FREE BOOKS!
2 FREE NOVELS PLUS 2 FREE GIFTS!

 Harlequin®

ROMANTIC
SUSPENSE
Sparked by Danger, Fueled by Passion.

YES! Please send me 2 FREE Harlequin® Romantic Suspense novels and my 2 FREE gifts (gifts are worth about $10). After receiving them, if I don't wish to receive any more books, I can return the shipping statement marked "cancel." If I don't cancel, I will receive 4 brand-new novels every month and be billed just $4.49 per book in the U.S. or $5.24 per book in Canada. That's a saving of at least 14% off the cover price! It's quite a bargain! Shipping and handling is just 50¢ per book in the U.S. and 75¢ per book in Canada.* I understand that accepting the 2 free books and gifts places me under no obligation to buy anything. I can always return a shipment and cancel at any time. Even if I never buy another book, the two free books and gifts are mine to keep forever.

240/340 HDN FEFR

Name _____ (PLEASE PRINT) _____

Address _____ Apt. # _____

City _____ State/Prov. _____ Zip/Postal Code _____

Signature (if under 18, a parent or guardian must sign) _____

Mail to the **Reader Service:**
IN U.S.A.: P.O. Box 1867, Buffalo, NY 14240-1867
IN CANADA: P.O. Box 609, Fort Erie, Ontario L2A 5X3

Not valid for current subscribers to Harlequin Romantic Suspense books.

Want to try two free books from another line?
Call 1-800-873-8635 or visit www.ReaderService.com.

* Terms and prices subject to change without notice. Prices do not include applicable taxes. Sales tax applicable in N.Y. Canadian residents will be charged applicable taxes. Offer not valid in Quebec. This offer is limited to one order per household. All orders subject to credit approval. Credit or debit balances in a customer's account(s) may be offset by any other outstanding balance owed by or to the customer. Please allow 4 to 6 weeks for delivery. Offer available while quantities last.

Your Privacy—The Reader Service is committed to protecting your privacy. Our Privacy Policy is available online at www.ReaderService.com or upon request from the Reader Service.

We make a portion of our mailing list available to reputable third parties that offer products we believe may interest you. If you prefer that we not exchange your name with third parties, or if you wish to clarify or modify your communication preferences, please visit us at www.ReaderService.com/consumerchoice or write to us at Reader Service Preference Service, P.O. Box 9062, Buffalo, NY 14269. Include your complete name and address.

HRS11B

Special excerpt from Harlequin Nocturne

*In a time of war between humans and vampires,
the only hope of peace lies in the love between
mortal enemies Captain Fiona Donnelly
and the deadly vampire scout Kain....*

*Read on for a sneak peek at "Halfway to Dawn"
by* New York Times *bestselling author Susan Krinard.*

* * *

Fiona opened her eyes.

The first thing she saw was the watery sunlight filtering through the waxy leaves of the live oak above her. The first thing she remembered was the bloodsuckers roaring and staggering about, drunk on her blood.

And then the sounds of violence, followed by quiet and the murmuring of voices. A strong but gentle touch. Faces...

Nightsiders.

No more than a few feet away, she saw two men huddled under the intertwined branches of a small thicket.

Vassals. That was what they had called themselves. But they were still Nightsiders. They wouldn't try to move until sunset. She could escape. All she had to do was find enough strength to get up.

"Fiona."

The voice. The calm baritone that had urged her to be still, to let him...

Her hand flew to her neck. It was tender, but she could feel nothing but a slight scar where the ugly wounds had been.

"Fiona," the voice said again. Firm but easy, like that of a man used to command and too certain of his own masculinity to fear compassion. The man emerged from the thicket.

He was unquestionably handsome, though there were deep shadows under his eyes and cheekbones. He wore only a shirt against the cold, a shirt that revealed the breadth of his shoulders and the fitness of his body. A soldier's body.

"It's all right," the man said, raising his hand. "The ones who attacked you are dead, but you shouldn't move yet. Your body needs more time."

"Kain," she said. "Your name is Kain."

He nodded. "How much do you remember?"

Too much, now that she was fully conscious. Pain, humiliation, growing weakness as the blood had been drained from her veins.

"Why did you save me? You said you were deserters."

"We want freedom," Kain said, his face hardening. "Just as you do."

Freedom from the Bloodlord or Bloodmaster who virtually owned them. But vassals still formed the majority of the troops who fought for these evil masters.

No matter what these men had done for her, they were still her enemies.

* * *

Discover the intense conclusion to
"Halfway to Dawn"
by Susan Krinard, featured in
HOLIDAY WITH A VAMPIRE 4,
available November 13, 2012,
from Harlequin® Nocturne™.

ROMANTIC SUSPENSE

Get your heart racing this holiday season with double the pulse-pounding action.

Christmas Confidential

Featuring

Holiday Protector by **Marilyn Pappano**

Miri Duncan doesn't care that it's almost Christmas. She's got bigger worries on her mind. But surviving the trip to Georgia from Texas is going to be her biggest challenge. Days in a car with the man who broke her heart and helped send her to prison—private investigator Dean Montgomery.

A Chance Reunion by **Linda Conrad**

When the husband Elana Novak left behind five years ago shows up in her new California home she knows danger is coming her way. To protect the man she is quickly falling for Elana must convince private investigator Gage Chance that she is a different person. But Gage isn't about to let her walk away…even with the bad guys right on their heels.

Available December 2012 wherever books are sold!

When legacy commands, these Greek royals must obey!

Discover a page-turning new Harlequin Presents® duet from *USA TODAY* bestselling author

Maisey Yates

A ROYAL WORLD APART

Desperate to escape an arranged marriage, Princess Evangelina has tried every trick in her little black book to dodge her security guards. But where everyone else has failed, will her new bodyguard bend her to his will…and steal her heart?

Available November 13, 2012.

AT HIS MAJESTY'S REQUEST

Prince Stavros Drakos rules his country like his business—with a will of iron! And when duty demands an heir, this resolute bachelor will turn his sole focus to the task….

But will he finally have met his match in a world-renowned matchmaker?

**Coming December 18, 2012,
wherever books are sold.**